It Had to Be Brew

Cheri Ritz

Praise for the works of Cheri Ritz

Under New Management

There are some twists and reveals that added complexity to our main character's journey... Because the path to love never runs smoothly! Overall, this was a fun and feelgood story that also included some amazing sounding Italian dishes. Be prepared to feel hungry!

-Leane, *NetGalley*

I liked the neighborhood feel of the story, and even the side characters were vibrant. I thought I knew where the story was going, but I was still surprised by the twist. I definitely recommend if you want a lighthearted foody romance. And now I'm craving Italian food...

-Jasmine S., *NetGalley*

An Acquired Taste

An Acquired Taste is very cute! I appreciated how sweet the romance is and I enjoyed spending time with these characters and watching them fall in love.

-The Lesbian Review

This is the first time I've read a book by Cheri Ritz, and I wasn't disappointed. ...This book was cute, with some funny moments. I found once started, it was difficult to put down, 'Just one more chapter' comes to mind.

-Cathy W., *NetGalley*

...Ms. Ritz has brought together two women that you will find yourself rooting for. Great characters and great supporting cast has made this a very entertaining read. Very, very good.

-Bonnie S., *NetGalley*

…The cooking in the book made me itch to start prepping, creating, cooking and eating. The visuals you get in your mind's eyes while Elle brought Ashley on a culinary learning journey were such a plus that you can literally smell and taste the food and of them falling in love. I thoroughly enjoyed the read as the book has the same satisfying end akin to a good meal that leaves you feeling upbeat, wholesome and all around happy.

-Nutmeg, *NetGalley*

Vacation People

The character work is solid, the relationship is developed well, and the settings seemed vivid. If you like vacation romances, you should pick up *Vacation People*. I'm looking forward to seeing more stories from Cheri Ritz in the future, because this was a great debut.

-The Lesbian Review

Other Bella Books by Cheri Ritz

Vacation People
Let the Beat Drop
Love's No Joke
Low Key Love
An Acquired Taste
Under New Management

About the Author

Cheri Ritz is a Pittsburgh native, wife, mom of 3, and author of several books published with Bella Books. She loves reading romance novels, so writing happily ever afters is a dream come true for her. She enjoys binge watching her favorite TV shows, crafting, and 80's and 90's pop culture. You can catch her around Pittsburgh trying new IPAs, hanging at home with her wife and two rambunctious cats, or working on her next novel.

It Had to Be Brew

Cheri Ritz

BELLA BOOKS

Bella Books, Inc.
P.O. Box 10543
Tallahassee, FL 32302

First Edition - 2025

Editor: Medora MacDougall
Cover Designer: SJ Hardy

ISBN: 978-1-64247-672-9

Acknowledgements

Thank you to Jessica and Linda Hill, and all the fine folks at Bella Books. I appreciate all you do to put these stories out into the world. Thank you also to my editor, Medora MacDougall. You took my little story about two gals and some craft beer and really made it shine!

Thanks to my dear friend Brooke Campbell for the writing sprints/gab sessions/writing retreats that help shape words into full stories. Let's keep it rolling! I also want to thank Maddie and Natasha for their willingness to bounce ideas and talk characters at all times of the day.

A heartfelt shout-out to my readers. If you've been on this book journey with me for a while, I appreciate you sticking around. If you're new to my books, I'm grateful you're here now. I truly love sharing my stories with you all.

I couldn't do this without the support of my family. Jaime—thanks for listening to me talk through plot points and for joining in on (many) impromptu brainstorm sessions. And my boys—hugs and kisses of thanks to you. You're all such a key part of this dream come true. xo

For Jaime

CHAPTER ONE

The last place Marigold Luxe expected to be at 3:43 a.m. Sunday morning was the Ritz-Carlton in downtown LA. But there she was, wearing the jeans she'd picked up off her floor when the phone rang, along with the threadbare Indigo Girls concert T-shirt she'd been sleeping in. At least she'd had the good sense to throw a blazer over it at the last minute. Now the concierge was marching her down a long hallway with ridiculously plush red-and-gold carpeting and shiny brass wall sconces dimmed to a lighting level appropriate for the early-morning hour.

She heard the reason for her arrival before she could even see the room number on the door placard.

"Do you not know who I am?" The loud words were slurred. "I'm Ava Ashford! Dakota Oakley?"

For most talent managers, extracting drunk clients from hotels in the wee hours of the morning wasn't a typical part of the job. But Marigold was known as the fixer at the agency where she was employed, and that meant going above and beyond for clients who needed special handling. And this time it meant being a big ol' 3 a.m. party pooper at the Ritz-Carlton.

Marigold fixed her face into a calm expression, bracing herself for what she would find on the other side of the door. She held steady, but inwardly she winced when the concierge pushed it open to reveal her indignant, nineteen-year-old client wearing wide-leg jeans and a bra, standing with fists on hips, facing off with the hotel's head night manager. The room was trashed—the sofa overturned, the floor littered with empty beer bottles and the passed-out partiers who had emptied them, and the large screen television mounted to the wall now featuring a huge spiderweb crack radiating from the center as if it had been used by Dakota Oakley for target practice.

"Seriously," Ava continued her rant, "you've never heard of *Homestead Hollow*? Lez ride!"

The line from the show was actually "let's ride," but due to the sapphic inclination of Ava's character, the fans had shifted her catch phrase to "lez ride" and it had stuck. To Marigold's disappointment, it had also recently been spray-painted in big, jet-black letters onto one of the hotel room's laurel-green walls.

"I assure you, miss, I have not," William, the manager attempting to mitigate the situation, said before turning to Marigold. "Ah, Ms. Luxe. Thank you for arriving so quickly."

"Thank you for calling me and not the police." She handed him her business card on top of a few hundred dollar bills. "The firm will pay for all damages just as soon as we receive an invoice. We appreciate your discretion." She handed the concierge a large tip as well.

"The only reason I did not alert the authorities was because the young lady gave me your name. We'd had numerous noise complaints about this room over the course of the night. When I finally came up here to investigate and found the suite in such a state..."

Marigold pulled two more bills from her back pocket and passed them to him under the guise of a grateful handshake. Unfortunately, this was not the first time she'd been called to the Ritz-Carlton to extract a rowdy client. "And I appreciate that, William. Give me a couple of minutes and we'll be out of your hair." She turned to Ava and changed her tone to reflect her displeasure. "Find your shirt."

Ava seemed to register that the party was over. While she walked the room looking for the rest of the outfit she'd started the evening in, Marigold and the concierge rousted the stragglers from their various states of coherence and directed them to the security guards who waited silently in the hallway to escort them off the premises.

"None of these other folks are mine, so if they give you any trouble go ahead and call the cops. I'll take this one with me." She linked her arm through Ava's to indicate she was officially on a short leash. "And thanks again, William."

"Of course." He gave her a curt nod and what she read as a hint of a sympathetic smile before retreating from the room.

* * *

"What the hell were you thinking?" Marigold had been driving for nearly ten minutes in silence before she couldn't stand it anymore.

Apparently Ava was fine without speaking during the drive. She sat slouched in the passenger seat, arms crossed, staring at her knees. Marigold actually preferred quiet Ava to the boisterous, drunken, braggadocious version from earlier. The thing was, she was expecting at the very least, a thank-you for what had just occurred. So she couldn't help poking.

"Okay, yeah. I know what you were thinking. 'I'm Ava Ashford. I'm a big freaking deal.' Right? But being on a popular television show doesn't give you the right to behave like a…like that." More silence. Marigold blew out an exasperated sigh. "I was sleeping, for heaven's sake. Why did you have them call me instead of your grandmother anyway?"

The question was met with a wry look and more silence.

"Yeah, I get it," Marigold said. "I wouldn't have wanted my grandma to walk into that scene if I were in your shoes."

"You missed the exit." Ava finally spoke.

"What?"

"To my house. You missed the exit to my house."

"I didn't *miss* it." Marigold kept her gaze trained on the road ahead of her. "I *passed* it. I'm taking you to my house to sleep this off. I don't need you expressing your Dakota Oakley enthusiasm any further this evening. I mean, this morning. I'll drive you home after some sleep and some breakfast. I don't want you out of my sight until I'm certain you've sobered up."

Ava leaned her head against the window of the passenger door. She looked like a sleepy little girl. Her single word was nearly inaudible. "Okay."

* * *

When Marigold woke the next morning, Ava Ashford was not slumbering on the sofa where she'd been left in the wee hours of the morning. The blankets were still on the couch, and the just-in-case puke bucket was beside it—thankfully empty—but Ava was nowhere to be found.

A quick check of the front door confirmed what she expected: it wasn't locked, the way she'd left it when she'd finally gone to bed only three hours earlier. *Thanks a lot for that, kid.*

She clicked the deadbolt back in place and rested her sleepy head against the door. "Damn it."

Then she spotted the note on the side table, scribbled on the back of an old food delivery receipt.

THANKS, MARIGOLD. - A.A.

CHAPTER TWO

Kasima Powell fixed a smile on her face and did her best to look interested as her brother rattled off sales figures, comparisons, and year-to-date goals. The news was all positive—even if she hadn't understood the numbers, she was able to tell that by his excited gesturing and the tinge of laughter in his voice.

She was glad the numbers brought Spencer so much joy. His focus on the sales side of the business freed her up to focus on the actual product, the beer. She preferred her role as head brewer at Enchanted Hops Brewing Company, the Powell family business in Montebello, just east of downtown LA. "And finally, one personal note before we wrap up." Spencer put his hands on his hips, all business despite the fact that he had declared this part of his spiel was personal. "Olivia asked me to remind everyone that even though we have the big SoCal Wildlife Rescue fundraiser next Friday night, Matty's birthday party is the Sunday after. Family members, you all said you would be there, so please show up. After all, a kid only turns eight once."

"Thanks, Spence."

All eyes turned to their father as he stood. He was dressed in his usual casual work clothes—jeans and a T-shirt with a zip vest over it. Dressing in layers was always a good idea in early March. Temperatures in various parts of the brewery campus could vary. As the CEO of Enchanted Hops and the one who led these weekly meetings, he would be the one to have the last word. Brian Powell led with kindness and grace, treating his team of employees with respect. Kasima admired him very much.

"Please assure Olivia that no one has forgotten about Matty's party. We're all excited to celebrate with him."

The big man's jovial expression may have relayed assurance that the event on Sunday was on his radar, but the way he quickly typed something into his phone tipped Kasima off. He was probably setting a reminder for himself, but he didn't need to worry. Her mom would never let him miss the event anyway.

"Okay, I think that's about it." Her father picked up the business thread, and while he made his closing remarks, Kasima gathered her belongings, ready to bolt as soon as they were officially dismissed. If she stuck around too long, she ran the risk of—

"Kasima, can I see you for a moment before you run off?"

Busted.

She slid from her chair and literally dragged her Doc Martens in her slow approach to her father. She knew what was coming, and there appeared to be no escape in sight. Perhaps deflection was called for.

"You know, Dad, I've been keeping a close eye on the oxygen levels in the old fermentation tanks. I'm worried some of the tanks might need replacing," she said, hugging her notebook to her chest and rocking on her thick-soled heels. Making it clear she was anxious to get back to work. "I want to give them a good look-over before I leave for the day."

"Yes, yes. I'm sure you'll take care of it." His gaze followed the last stragglers as they left the conference room. The moment it was just the two of them, he placed a meaty but gentle hand on her shoulder and his tone changed to that of a concerned father.

"Spencer will have Olivia at the fundraiser on Friday, and I'll have your mother. It would be nice to see you there with a date instead of taking everything on as a solo act. I know you're a strong, independent woman, and that's great. I love that about you. But your mom and I worry about you. You're always alone. It's been over five years since—"

"I have a date for Friday," Kasima interrupted in an overly bright tone. "You don't have to worry, I will not be alone at the fundraiser, because I have a date. A date for the fundraiser."

"You have a date for Friday?" His expression went the whole range of dad emotions, from confused to surprised to something like delight. "You have a date for Friday. That's great, Kas."

"Yep, no need to worry about that, so I'm gonna go check on those tanks."

She gave him a quick peck on the cheek before hurrying off to the fermentation tanks. She wasn't proud that she'd lied to her father. Not about the oxygen levels in the old tanks—they were suspect, but she would keep a close eye on them and get them serviced if needed. The part about having a date for the fundraiser, though—total lie. She didn't feel good about that at all. But she just couldn't bear to play another round of, "It's been five years since…" with a family member. Or with anyone, really. She was fine, and she would reenter the dating scene when she was good and ready. Today wasn't that day. She was beginning to believe that day might never come, and she was prepared to make her peace with that. Her family, though…that would be a tougher battle.

As she walked the cement floor of the warehouse that served as a dank farm for the old fermentation tanks, she stopped to carefully note the oxygen levels on each one. No change from earlier. Maybe they were fine and what she'd seen earlier was a fluke, but she'd check back regularly to make sure there wasn't a problem. They wouldn't lose all that product on her watch. She was much too good a brewer to let that happen.

An issue with the old tanks she could handle, no sweat. Finding a date for the fundraiser to make the lie she'd told her dad into a truth—that was a whole other story.

CHAPTER THREE

The Saturday after the Ritz-Carlton incident Marigold was at her best friend Elle's wedding, trying to enjoy the party. She and Elle had known each other since they were kids and costars on the teen drama *Sugar & Spice*. They'd remained close even after the show went off the air and Marigold quit acting and went to college. She eventually returned to show business, only on the management side of things this time. In fact, Elle had been participating in a reality TV cooking competition that Marigold had booked for her when she met her bride, Ashley. Marigold should be relaxing and basking in their special day with them, but instead she was worrying all the while that she was going to receive another 911 call from Ava Ashford.

At Elle's insistence, she'd turned the ringer of her phone off for the entirety of the ceremony, and she'd been quite relieved after it to discover no missed texts or calls. As the beautiful backyard reception began, though, she was very aware that her evening off could be interrupted at any minute. Things had been quiet for the first couple of days after the hotel incident, but Ava's silence hadn't lasted for long. On Wednesday morning she'd called Marigold with a thirty-minute diatribe about how she wanted worked into the contract for any appearances she made that there would be a large bowl of jelly beans in her dressing room, but the bowl must not contain any yellow jelly beans because she "hay-ay-ates" yellow jelly beans. Then on Thursday she showed up at the office unannounced, plopped down on the sofa in Marigold's office, ordered in a mani/pedi service and lunch, and then proceeded to enjoy these treats right there in Marigold's office—before finally slipping away while Marigold was in the restroom, leaving the McClancy-Jansen Agency to pick up the tab for the whole shebang. This client was really pushing the limits of her nerves. It was ridiculous.

But today was not about clients, she reminded herself. It was about friends. Celebrating Elle and Ashley.

Mid-March was the perfect time in Southern California for an outdoor wedding. Rainy season was over. The temperature was warm, but not so hot that guests would be uncomfortable in their semiformal attire. It was sunny and comfortable, which, if you threw in a dash of class, was basically the brides' whole aesthetic. Elle had been Marigold's best friend forever, and Ashley—Elle's beautiful bride—was simply lovely and charming. She and Marigold had become fast friends as well. Their wedding was truly a happy day all around.

Marigold edged away from the dancing crowd, shimmying her shoulders the whole time in hopes nobody would notice her escape. She needn't have worried. As soon as the song changed and the opening beats of "The Cupid Shuffle" bumped from the speakers, a wave of partygoers abandoned their tables and swarmed the dance floor, suddenly ready to dance the night away.

"I've always said there are few things queer women love more than 'The Cupid Shuffle,'" she muttered as she sidled up to the bar. Perhaps a beer would help her relax.

"Definitely right up there with flannel shirts and power tools," the pretty bartender with kind eyes confirmed. "What can I get you?"

The mobile bar was fashioned from a vintage silver horse trailer refurbished to be a bar on wheels, lit with fairy lights and decorated with romantic swags of greenery. A service window had been cut in the side with a drop-down counter that served as the bar. The bartender leaned through it, resting on her very sexy and muscular forearms. It took Marigold a moment to stop gawping and form words.

"I, uh…" *Look at the woman's face, dammit.* When Marigold finally lifted her gaze, it was met by a winsome smile. The bartender had a girl-next-door look about her that made you feel right at home. "I'll try a La La Land Lager."

"Coming right up." She pushed off the counter to pour the drink from an amber growler.

While she worked, Marigold reread the names of the beer options written in bright colors on the chalkboard menu and couldn't suppress her smile. Sunset Brewavard, Wizard of Haze. Someone had put a lot of thought into the brewery's theme.

"Those names are so clever," she said as she accepted her full glass. "I really like Mead West."

"Right? It's my favorite too." She leaned in and stage-whispered in a conspiratorial tone, "I made that one up myself."

"They let the bartenders name the beers?" Marigold asked, wiping some beer foam from her lip with the back of her hand. "That's mighty nice of them."

"They do when you're also the head brewer." She laughed and stuck out a hand to shake. "Kasima Powell. My family owns Enchanted Hops Brewing Company located in Montebello. My dad is nuts about movies, hence the brew names."

"Marigold Luxe." She took the offered hand, holding on a beat longer than she should have. Kasima's firm grasp was tempered by her soft skin, and her friendly demeanor was enhanced by the flecks of gold in her deep brown eyes. She had a dreamy quality to her that Marigold found just as enchanting as the beer Kasima brewed. "Talent manager. And friend of the brides."

"Makes sense. The friend of the brides thing, I mean." Kasima pulled a bar towel from her belt loop and wiped some condensation from the bar. "So, how come you aren't out there cutting a rug to the line dance beloved by sapphics everywhere? You don't date women?"

"Marigold doesn't date anyone," Elle Bissett deadpanned from over Marigold's shoulder. Her best friend had perfect timing, as usual. "She's much too busy agenting to date."

"Ha, ha. I'm only taking your abuse because it's your wedding day," Marigold joked back, her cheeks going hot with embarrassment that Kasima now knew she had absolutely no social life. "I do, in fact, date women." *Smooth.*

"Good to know." Kasima never lost that smile. She'd probably made a killing in tips chatting up the wedding guests and flashing those dimples. Good for her. "What's the bride drinking?"

"I'll try the Hollywood Haze."

While Kasima was busy grabbing another growler of beer, Marigold turned to Elle. "What are you trying to do to me here? We were having a conversation." She lowered her voice to avoid being overheard. "I find her quite interesting."

"Don't worry. That was obvious from the way you threw in that last part—the 'I do, in fact, date women,'" Elle joked, spot-on with her imitation of Marigold's voice. That was what you got when your best friend of nearly twenty years was also a talented voice actor. "Besides, I was merely stating the facts. I seriously can't remember the last time you had a date."

"Maybe I just didn't tell you." Marigold's retort was an empty one, but it was punctuated with a sharp look meant to indicate Elle should zip it since Kasima was returning with the beer.

Elle either didn't notice the look or didn't care. "For the record," she said to Kasima, "I stand corrected. Mari *might* be dating; she's just not telling anyone."

"Good heavens, Elle. Don't you have a new bride to go dance with?" Marigold murmured, trying her damnedest to ignore the amused look sparkling in Kasima's beautiful brown eyes, but it was so very hard to look away from them. "The truth is, I've been a little busy at work lately, and I haven't had much time for dating."

Beside her Elle cleared her throat loudly.

"Fine." Marigold sighed. "I've been busy at work for the past couple years, so I haven't had much time for dating."

"At least a couple years," Elle pointed out.

"Okay, you've made your point," Marigold relented. She wasn't going to save face in front of Kasima at this point anyway. "My job *is* demanding, but I'm damn good at it. I haven't been on a date in forever, but I don't expect work is going to slow down anytime soon, so…" She shrugged. "I miss going out, but I'm too busy to be a good partner to anybody. Romance just isn't in the cards for me right now."

"Oh, that's sad." Elle frowned dramatically and shook her head. "Poor Mari. Isn't that just the saddest thing you've heard all night?" she asked Kasima, who had gone back to wiping down the bar.

"Don't do that," Marigold said between gulps of beer. She was used to Elle's penchant for banter, and she knew how to play the game. "Don't drag Kasima into it. She's just trying to do her job."

"Please don't worry about me." Kasima jumped in without missing a beat. "This isn't even really my job. I'm doing someone else's job. On a Saturday night no less. I'm in no position to judge someone for working too much. Besides…" She returned the towel to her belt loop and leaned across the bar. "I think I have an idea that will get you out for a date with absolutely no strings attached and help me out in the meantime."

"I'm intrigued," Elle piped up.

"She means me, not you, blushing bride." Marigold stuck her tongue out at her best friend before turning back to Kasima. "I'm also intrigued."

"I need a date for a fundraiser Enchanted Hops is involved with next week. Friday. Would you like to be my date?" Kasima asked, quickly adding, "It would totally be a one-time only thing, of course. Just so I can get my parents off my back regarding my singleton status at yet another company event. We can get all dressed up, eat some fancy food, maybe take a spin around the dance floor to make us look legit. What do you say?"

A real night out including fancy food and semiformal wear sounded pretty enticing. Especially the part about no-strings attached. For once she could enjoy an evening out with a woman without the nagging feeling that her date would be expecting romance to bloom only for her to end up a woman scorned when Marigold's work schedule inevitably got in the way of their Happily Ever After ever getting off the ground. But there was one part of this proposition that was giving her pause.

"A fancy fundraiser sounds appealing," Marigold admitted. "But I'm sure a woman like you has no problem getting dates. Why are you asking a total stranger to be your date?"

Was it her imagination or did the other woman's smile falter for a moment?

Kasima paused and seemed to take a deep breath before responding with a shrug, "Like you said before—romance just isn't in the cards for me either right now. But if I show up to the fundraiser arm-in-arm with a beautiful woman, it will definitely appease my parents. At least for a while."

Marigold's cheeks went warm at the compliment thrown into the answer. Apparently, it hadn't gone unnoticed by Elle either.

"Aw, come on." Elle grinned like the Cheshire Cat. "How can you say no to that? I, for one, think this is a great idea. Go out and have some fun for a change."

"I'll take that under advisement," Marigold said. "Why don't you go back to your bride and let Kasima and me work this out?"

Elle held up her hands in surrender as she backed away from the bar, but when she turned to walk away, she called over her shoulder, "Say yes, Mari."

Is this what it had come to? Picking up a date at the bar at Elle and Ashley's wedding? Of course, as Kasima had made clear, this wouldn't be an actual date. More like a fake one. No hearts would be broken in the making of this date. Kasima was still looking at her expectantly and possibly even hopefully.

"Okay. I'll be your date."

The way Kasima's expression relaxed back into that easy smile set off a flurry of butterflies in Marigold's belly, and she had to remind them to chill out. This was just going to be a fake date, after all.

* * *

After towing the mobile bar back to Enchanted Hops, unloading it, and locking up the shed where it was stored, Kasima climbed into her Jeep and started navigating the drive around the brewery toward the main road. The wedding had ended at nine, but with the packing up and the drive, it was after ten when she'd returned to the brewery. Her body was tired from tending bar all evening, but her mind was wide awake and whirling away. She couldn't believe her luck at solving her fundraiser date problem. Marigold Luxe was easy to talk to, she was even easier on the eyes, and based on the powder-blue wrap dress she'd worn to the wedding—the one that hugged her curves in all the right places—she knew how to dress for a semiformal event. All together it added up to the perfect date.

Fake date, she corrected herself.

As she steered the Jeep past the building closest to the road, the one that housed the Enchanted Hops Taproom, she noticed something she'd missed on her way in—her father's truck in the parking lot.

She'd put in a full day of work on her day off, but since her brain wasn't going to let her rest any time soon anyway, she decided it wouldn't hurt to go in, grab a beer, and see what was going on. Behind the bar she helped herself to a Tinseltown IPA before approaching the four-top by the big front window where her parents were seated.

"What are you two doing here?" Kasima asked, lowering herself into one of the chairs on the opposite side of the table from them. "And both sitting on the same side of the table—that's weird."

"Oh, honey, it's not weird." Her mom tsk-tsked at her, but her sweet smile kept her tone from sounding like an actual scolding. "We came here with the Petersons for a drink and a snack after bowling. You just missed them."

"And I was telling your mother that you were bringing a date to the fundraising event next weekend," her father added brightly. "What did you say her name was?"

She hadn't, of course, because when she'd told her father that she didn't actually *have* a date. A silent thank-you was sent up to the stars for the serendipity she'd been blessed with earlier in the evening. "It's Marigold."

"Marigold," her mom repeated. "That's an unusual name."

Her dad drained the last of the beer in his glass. "Any girlfriend of Kasima's is bound to be extraordinary."

Girlfriend? Oh geez. That escalated quickly. Kasima took a fortifying gulp of beer.

"I didn't know you had a girlfriend." Disappointment at being left out of the loop was written across her mom's face. "I didn't even know you were dating again."

"Well, it just sort of happened," Kasima said. "Suddenly." She was a terrible liar.

Her mom's expression brightened, and she grasped her husband's hand. "You have a girlfriend! This is wonderful news."

"I, for one, cannot wait to meet her." Her father beamed.

The situation was going off the rails fast, but if Kasima corrected her parents now and told them Marigold wasn't actually her girlfriend, those happy, hopeful faces would turn back into the ones full of worry and pity that had appeared anytime the subject of Kasima and dating had come up over the past few years. She was tired—both of those sad looks and from the day of tending bar. She didn't need to take this small joy away from them—not tonight. What could a little white lie possibly hurt?

She fixed her face into a smile and said, "You'll meet her Friday at the fundraiser."

CHAPTER FOUR

Monday morning Marigold met with her boss for a routine update on her roster of clients, but mostly it was a rundown of Ava Ashford's latest outrageous demands and questionable behavior.

"I realize that a middle-of-the-night phone call and client rescue mission is an inconvenience, but you did good work last week, Marigold." Allison Jansen was a legacy partner at McClancy-Jansen Management, the talent agency where Marigold had worked her entire career. Allison's father, Richard Jansen, had been a founding partner. When he retired last year, she had slid nice and easy into his corner office.

Marigold missed Richard Jansen.

"The kid's a mess. She's getting a little too big for her britches, if you ask me." Marigold shifted in her seat. She should have remained standing for this meeting. She was pretty sure Allison purposely selected the hardest, most uncomfortable chairs in the world to set opposite her desk with the intention of keeping her visitors off-kilter. "Expect an invoice from the hotel. And I'll start working on appearances for Ava to offset any bad press that's yet to hit. We might want to think about keeping her busy for a while—keep her out of trouble. At least public trouble."

Allison glanced at something on her phone, then took a long sip from the delicate teacup she insisted on using instead of the McClancy-Jansen Management-branded mugs everyone else in the office drank from. Extended awkward silences—another one of her superpowers. "Let's not make her feel as if we're restricting her. We want to keep the client happy."

"Restricting her? She—an underage girl, by the way—drank her weight in tequila, invited a bunch of strangers to her hotel room, and then proceeded to trash it. I'm simply asking that we encourage her to behave like a responsible member of society and not give in to every whim that drifts across her still-adolescent mind. I would think you would be a fan of keeping it classy."

Allison merely shot her a look that indicated she wasn't dignifying that last bit with a response.

"Come on," Marigold tried again, her frustration with her boss rising. "The girl is acting like a total brat. I think we need to rein her in before she does something that is a step too far. Something she can't come back from."

"Total brat behavior or not, Ava is right about one thing." Allison sat up straighter in her chair. Her mind was clearly made up and her word was law. "She's on her way to becoming really big. She's certainly not there yet, but this Dakota Oakley role could do it for her if the show's viewership continues to grow. The queer community loves her, and they are a very strong fanbase, but *Homestead Hollow* has mainstream television appeal too. Bottom line, Ava's rising star is our rising star as long as we keep her as a client. So I want you to do whatever it takes to keep her as a client while you manage her career. I'm talking kid-glove treatment here."

Marigold opened her mouth to protest, but Allison held up a hand to stop her.

That's all," Allison said, this time without looking up from her phone. She'd delivered her message and Marigold was dismissed. Their weekly meeting was done.

It was against her gut feeling for how to handle the situation, but a kid-glove strategy for managing Ava Ashford it would be. Best to just get back to her own office and tend to her other clients before the Ava drama kicked up for the week anyway.

CHAPTER FIVE

Kasima stood at the front door of Marigold's Pacific Palisades bungalow, rang the bell, and shifted her weight from foot to foot. She was already regretting her decision to wear heels instead of her usual Doc Martens. Maybe she could ask the driver to swing by her place on the way to the event so she could change or at least grab a pair as a backup. Before she could weigh the pros and cons of comfortable shoes versus arriving late to her father's table at the fundraiser, the door opened.

"Hi. Oh my God." Marigold had halted just two steps outside of her doorway. "When you said you were taking a car to pick me up, I assumed it would be some kind of Uber situation, not this." She gestured at the sleek black Cadillac idling at the curb. "Very fancy."

"Believe me, I'm much more of a Jeep kind of gal, but my dad insists on going all out for these kinds of events. My family is big on celebrations. They have a…joy for life you could say. Is your family like that?"

"No," Marigold said simply as she ducked into the back seat of the car.

Kasima slid in beside her, expecting her to expand on that answer. She didn't. But Kasima wasn't going to let that stop her from digging for additional information. She was feeling too anxious to sit quietly for the ride. She wasn't proud of the way she'd lied to her family—it was weighing on her conscience. The fact was, Marigold was coming with her to the event, so it wasn't a total lie that she was her date. Technically. But she'd taken it too far when she was talking to her dad. She'd gotten swept up in his excitement on her behalf. She should have just corrected him when he used the word "girlfriend," and nipped it in the bud. But she hadn't. Now she had to worry that something would go sideways tonight and she would end up totally embarrassing herself in front of this perfectly lovely woman who had merely agreed to attend a fundraiser with her.

"I would think a television star such as yourself would be accustomed to this sort of thing, Miss *Sugar & Spice*."

"You recognized me? That was twenty years ago."

"My memory was assisted by Google," Kasima admitted.

"You Googled me?" The sparkle in Marigold's forest-green eyes made it clear her shocked look was in jest.

"Of course I did. I'm about to introduce you to my whole family at an event that is important to our business. I had to make sure you weren't some kind of extreme right-wing weirdo or something," Kasima teased back. "Thirty-seven years old, graduate of USC, on the donor list of the Human Rights Campaign. You passed the test."

"The Google test? That's a pretty low bar you hold for potential dates."

"*Fake* dates," Kasima quickly corrected.

"Fake dates," Marigold repeated. Her gaze dropped to the black clutch purse in her lap, and she fidgeted with the clasp. "Either way, I'm relieved I passed the test."

Had she said something wrong? Kasima studied the woman sitting beside her. Marigold's A-line cocktail dress was the perfect combination of elegant and sexy and was most likely designer.

The dark navy shade somehow made her auburn hair even more striking. There was no doubt she looked the part of the perfect date. More importantly, they'd had such an easy rapport chatting at the wedding last week, Kasima couldn't help but like her. Marigold was exactly the kind of woman she would be interested in dating—*if* she was interested in dating at all. Regardless, she hadn't meant to make the moment awkward, and she wanted to get the night back on track. She placed a light hand on Marigold's forearm. "You very much did. Thank you for doing this. I promise we'll have a fun night."

Marigold's expression brightened again, and she was back to being the confident woman Kasima recognized from their first meeting.

"As Elle pointed out last week, I desperately needed a night out—and a break from work—so I should be thanking you."

"We'll call it even then." Kasima was relieved to be back on even ground. "Tell me something about what you do. I think working with celebrities sounds very glamorous."

Marigold's laugh was a joyful blast. "It does sound glamorous. Unfortunately, usually it's not so much. Some of my clients can be challenging, and my office hours are basically twenty-four seven, but I get to stretch my creativity and I meet a lot of interesting people. It's hard work, but I have to admit, I love my job."

It was a sentiment Kasima could relate to and it further cemented her esteem for Marigold. "I get that. I feel the same way about my job. I feel really lucky that I love what I do for a living."

Before the discussion could go deeper, the car rolled to a stop. They'd reached their destination.

"Are you ready for this?" Kasima asked.

"I don't know if you've heard, but I used to be a professional actor." Marigold gave her a wink as the driver opened the door for them. "I'm totally ready to play the role of perfect date."

* * *

The historic Art Deco bank in downtown LA's Arts District made for a stunning venue for a fundraising event. The architecture and decor kept Marigold's head on a swivel as she attempted to take it all in as they wound their path through the cocktail-hour crowd toward the bar. It had been Kasima's idea to grab a drink before facing the Powell clan, and despite her bold boast about being a professional actor, Marigold was glad she had agreed. Playing a part on a television show was one thing. Lying to someone's parents was something else entirely. She didn't care for pretending to be something she wasn't when it came to real life. Never had. But this was just for one night, and she was dressed up and on the arm of Kasima—metaphorically for the moment anyway—at the event, so this could technically be a date and not a lie. Even if Kasima was dead set against admitting as much.

"Looks like we're jumping right in." Kasima handed her a glass of chardonnay and nodded in the direction of four people making a beeline for them.

"You're drinking wine and not beer?" Marigold eyed the glass Kasima was holding and pressed her free hand to her chest as if she was clutching pearls. "Will your family be upset? Isn't that against some kind of brewmaster rule?"

"Ha ha," Kasima joked back, but she looked distracted by the approaching group.

Marigold took a sip of wine and braced herself to meet the Powell family, but her worry turned out to be unwarranted. Kasima quickly introduced her all around—to her parents, who insisted she call them Brian and Julie, and to her brother, Spencer, and his wife, Olivia, noting that Marigold was a talent manager for McClancy-Jansen and former star of TV's *Sugar & Spice*. They were friendly and boisterous, and Marigold liked them right away.

The group chatted for a few minutes before Brian suggested they find their table and sit. He was a big, sturdy man—easily over six feet tall—with a ring of brown hair on his mostly bald head, and as he led his family through the crowd, he greeted many of the other attendees with an affable smile, handshakes, and affectionate slaps on their backs. It seemed he knew nearly everyone in the room.

Julie was equally gracious as they greeted the friends and acquaintances they passed. She had the same ash-brown hair as

Kasima, only with a few silver-gray streaks, and it was obvious Kasima got her round eyes and high cheekbones from her. When they reached their designated table, Julie selected her seat first, then indicated with a nod that Kasima and Marigold should take the chairs to her right.

The conversation immediately returned to the comfortable feeling they'd shared over cocktails and continued that way throughout dinner.

"How long has Enchanted Hops Brewing been partnered up with SoCal Wildlife Rescue?" Marigold asked as they dug into the dessert course. "I think it's a wonderful cause."

"I started our brewery in 2001, when Kasima was just eleven and Spencer was fifteen. I wanted to build a family business for all of us," Brian explained. "The very next year—after we were up and running and I was sure we had our feet under us—I reached out to the wildlife rescue folks. It only seemed right to give back to Mother Earth in some way since we were producing a product here. Kasima was a real animal lover when she was a kid, so SoCal Wildlife Rescue seemed to make sense."

"I think that's a wonderful reason," Marigold said before placing a gentle hand on top of Kasima's. "I'm an animal lover too. I've always been a fan of the big cats we have in our region. For my money, the beautiful and proud mountain lion can't be beat."

"The proud mountain lion is scary as hell." Kasima laughed. "I was more enamored with smaller creatures—opossum, raccoons, owls. That sort of thing."

"Some of those owls can be downright scary too. The way their heads do that *Exorcist* three-sixty swivel." Marigold shuddered. "Creepy."

"Anyway," Brian said with a warm smile that indicted he had been studying their exchange with amusement. "Last year was the first year we brewed a special beer for the cause and donated the proceeds to the group in addition to the other work we do with them. The special release was all Kasima's idea, and it was extremely successful."

"I'm a beer lover as well as an animal lover, so I think that's a great idea. Good for you." Marigold nodded her approval. "It's a smart way to raise money and get community involved in the cause. I love it."

"A beer lover, huh?" Brian's eyes lit up. "Maybe you can help Kasima out with picking a beer to brew for this year's special release. We need to start brewing it soon if we want to be able to get it on the market in late spring. It's a limited release, but we'll sell it all through the summer. Last year she had Spencer's assistance, but he's been so busy coaching his son's inline hockey team, he's kind of left her to fly solo on the project this time around and—"

"Geez, Dad. Marigold is a busy woman. She doesn't have time to sit around yapping about beer." Kasima swiftly cut him off.

"Actually," Marigold began her protest, but right at that moment, the president of SoCal Wildlife Rescue took the podium and began the program.

While he thanked sponsors and donors, Marigold used the time to observe Kasima. When she opened her door that evening and saw Kasima in that slinky jumpsuit, it was all she could do to keep her hands to herself. She'd had an incredible urge to run them over the champagne-hued satin. Instead of the braids Kasima had worn while serving beer at the wedding, her hair hung in loose, shoulder-length ringlets. And rounding out the outfit were peekaboo heels. The overall effect was damn sexy. She had redirected her excitement toward the car that would be ferrying them to the event, but she'd suspected Kasima hadn't been totally fooled. She needed to tamp down her attraction since Kasima had made it clear she wasn't interested in dating. Unless... maybe she would change her mind now that they'd spent some time together? They'd been getting along fine; there hadn't even been a single lull in the conversation. It all felt comfortable, but at the same time excitement hummed in Marigold's belly. It really seemed like there could be something between them, so why not?

The formal SoCal Wildlife Rescue presentation came to an end with one last pitch for donations, then plenty of applause from the crowd which dissipated as the deejay in the back corner of the event space started the music again. Marigold made a mental note to make an online pledge to the cause when she got home.

Brian and Spencer returned from the bar with another round of drinks for the table and the conversation resumed as Kasima told a story about a birthday party held in the brewery's taproom a few months earlier.

"And that's why our special events contract now contains a strict 'no glitter or confetti' clause," she concluded.

"It was such a mess," Spencer chimed in. "I swear, for weeks I was finding glitter in my—" He stopped midthought and his eyes went wide with what looked like mirth and his gaze slid from one family member to the next.

"Dad, you didn't!" Kasima gasped and held a hand up to her ear. "They're playing our song."

"They're playing your what now?" Marigold recognized the opening strains of an old disco song, but she was unsure exactly what it was the members of the Powell family were telegraphing to one another with their pointed looks.

"I totally did." Brian grinned at his daughter. "Come on, kids. Let's do it."

While Kasima and her family stood and began swaying in time to the beat. Marigold looked to her for clarification. "What is happening here?"

"Family dance," Kasima said like it was the most obvious answer in the world. "'We Are Family.' Get it? You can join us if you want."

Family dance? Was that a thing?

"I think I'll just observe this one." Marigold raised her glass in a salute. "Go enjoy."

Kasima gave her a little wave, her fingers wagging in time with the music, and sang along as she followed her mother to the dance floor. "We are fam-i-lee!"

Marigold sipped her wine and looked on while the Powells took over the small and otherwise empty dance floor. At first, she thought their dancing was best described as chaotic freestyle, but then the chorus hit and they shifted into a choreographed routine of claps, kicks, and hip gyrations. The thing that struck her most as they boogied down was the pure joy on each of their faces. All five of them were smiling and laughing and clearly having a very good time. The way Brian and Julie looked at each other with such love was touching and tugged at Marigold's heart. This family truly had something special.

The Powell family's contagious glee had Marigold tapping her foot and swaying in her seat. As the tune slid toward the chorus for the second time, the Powells turned to the folks still seated at tables watching them and gestured for them to join the fun. Kasima danced over to Marigold and pulled her onto the dance floor. This time she didn't resist.

Marigold did her best to mimic the choreography the others were performing—getting at least most of the stomps and claps in the right places—and bubbled over with laughter the whole time.

When the song ended the room broke out in applause and cheers. Kasima wrapped her arms around her. "You did great."

Marigold was surprised by the hug, but not at all put off by it. Being held in Kasima's strong arms felt like the most normal thing in the world and filled her with warmth. "Thanks. I've never been part of a family dance before."

While the group ambled back to the other table, a wide smile graced Brian's face. His pride in their family was evident. "That was just a warmup for Sunday. Matty's going to be so mad he missed it this time."

Marigold looked to Kasima to interpret.

"Matty's my nephew—Spencer's son. He's having his birthday party at a roller rink on Sunday," she explained. "He's turning eight."

"Oh, wow, roller-skating." Marigold couldn't remember the last time she'd dared to attempt the activity, but it brought to mind her preteen days. "That should be fun."

"You should join us, Marigold," Brian said with a look of delight.

The offer was tempting. Marigold was having more fun on this night out than she'd had in as long as she could remember, and one more outing with this group certainly wasn't objectionable. Still, this was supposed to be a one-night gig with Kasima. As it was she would be working most of Saturday to make up for the administrative tasks she'd neglected when she left the office early to dress for the fundraiser. Plus she didn't want to overstep. "I couldn't possibly intrude on a family celebration."

"Nonsense," he boomed. "The more the merrier!"

Again, Marigold looked to Kasima for guidance on the subject.

"There will be cake." Kasima shrugged. "How can you resist that?"

"Cake does make it pretty hard to say no," Marigold laughed. "Let me see how much work I get done tomorrow. I'll try my best to make it."

"Attagirl." Brian pumped a fist in approval before turning to the others at the table. "Okay, who needs a drink?"

Kasima leaned close and quietly said, "If you don't want to come to the party, that's fine. I won't hold you to anything—you only agreed to this one night and I know my family can be a little…overwhelming." Her warm breath against Marigold's neck triggered a shiver down her spine.

Marigold chuckled softly, hoping Kasima would think it was in response to the remark about her family and not to cover up her body's reaction to their proximity. First the hug, now this. "No, your family is great. And I'm truly having fun tonight. I'll really try to make it Sunday."

Before sitting up in her seat again, Kasima gave Marigold's hand a squeeze. The touch set off a heat that quickly spread through her whole body. Her brain reminded her that this was all pretend, but her body was too hopeful to accept it unconditionally. She could hang out with Kasima just one more time.

What could it hurt?

CHAPTER SIX

Marigold stepped into Sandville Skateland, and her senses were immediately assaulted. Excessively loud pop music was punctuated by bleeps and dings of arcade games, the disco ball hanging over the rink, coupled with the flashing beams of red and blue LED lights overhead, caused her eyes to water, and the air was filled with the smell of popcorn coupled with the sugary sweetness of cotton candy and rank undertones of…was that sweaty feet? Still, the sensory memory came rushing back—these were the same sensations she had experienced as a preteen on the rare occasion she was allowed to go to roller-skating. She stood just inside the entranceway, holding the remote-control monster truck she'd wrapped in colorful paper, and took it all in. It was vibrant and loud and…totally overwhelming.

What the hell was she doing at an eight-year-old's birthday party at a roller rink? She didn't even know the kid. Sure, his aunt was a pretty woman who was easy to talk to and fun to hang out with, but when you got right down to it, she didn't really know Kasima either. It's not like they were actually dating. And really, she still had work to catch up on. She could just text Kasima later with an apology and an excuse and that would be that. She'd done what she'd originally agreed to—been Kasima's date for the fundraiser. There was no reason to carry on this charade any longer.

"Marigold! I'm so glad you came." The booming voice stopped her retreating steps.

It was Kasima's dad, Brian, with a big, friendly smile and arms open wide as if ready to greet her with a bear hug. To her surprise, she found that idea comforting. But instead of giving her an embrace, he reached for the big box she was holding. "Let me take that for you. Come on, I'll show you where we're set up."

She followed him past a wall lined with pinball machines and a bay of bright orange metal lockers to an alcove with a neon sign that read "Party Room" above the entrance. He deposited the gift on a table covered by a plastic balloon-print tablecloth before announcing, "Look, everyone. Marigold's here."

Kasima looked up from where she was kneeling in front of two little kids, fussing with the laces on their skates. Presumably one of them was the birthday boy. Her chestnut-brown eyes went wide along with her smile when their gazes met. Damn, those dimples were adorable; they made Marigold more than glad she'd stayed for the party.

Kasima hopped up and sent the kids on their way. "Hey, thanks for coming." That beautiful smile remained on her lips. She introduced her to her nephew, Matty, and Marigold said hello to Spencer and his wife, Olivia, both of whom she remembered from the SoCal Wildlife Rescue fundraiser a couple of nights earlier. "Let me grab my skates and we'll get you a pair too."

"I'm going to feel silly in rented skates when you're wearing those beauties," Marigold said when she saw Kasima's pink glittery ones. "You must be quite a skater."

"Me? I guess I hold my own." Kasima grinned as they headed toward the rental window. "Matty's the real pro. He's obsessed with inline hockey. Learned to skate when he was four. This is actually the third year in a row he's had his birthday party here. Last year I decided to really get in the spirit of things and treated myself to a fancy pair of skates." She shrugged. "All the kids seem to get a kick out of an adult zooming around the rink in them."

"Zooming. Impressive." Marigold told the attendant her shoe size. Was she in over her head agreeing to hit the rink? "I feel like I should warn you. I haven't skated since the early aughts."

"Not a rink rat as a teen?"

Marigold laughed. "I wish. While all the other kids were blissfully couple skating on Friday nights, I was running lines and taking dance lessons. Back when I was acting, my mother was my manager. She very much frowned upon me doing anything that could result in broken bones. Putting on skates was a definite no-no. I was only allowed to go to the rink a handful of times. The result of which is, I'm not the most confident on wheels."

Kasima gave Marigold's shoulder a reassuring squeeze. "Don't worry, I got you."

Ten minutes later, Kasima was putting those words into action as the two made their first tentative lap of the rink.

Marigold teetered on her wheels, arms spread stiffly at her sides in an attempt to provide balance, while Kasima patiently kept her slow pace, occasionally circling her to stretch her skating chops.

"Hold your own, my ass," Marigold cracked. "You're going backward with much more grace than I have going forward."

"You're doing great."

She appreciated Kasima's support, but as a pack of second graders whizzed past her seeming to be so comfortable on wheels that they looked like they were born that way, she felt a fresh wave of doubt wash over her.

"If you want to do a few normal laps instead of babysitting me, I won't blame you one bit," Marigold said, drawing her torso up to appear more confident as they eased into the straight stretch on the far side of the rink. "Seriously, I'll be fine."

She probably would've been more believable if she hadn't had to flap her arms to keep balance as she finished the sentence.

Kasima seemed to bite back a laugh, and those dimples flashed again. This time the wobble in Marigold's knees had nothing to do with the wheels strapped to her feet.

"I'm quite content right here skating with you," Kasima said simply. "I'm glad you came to the party."

When Marigold cast a quick glance over at Kasima—who had chosen that moment to do a three-sixty spin—she was surprised to find that she was glad she came too. She was about to say as much when a group of four preteens all holding hands skated by. They were moving at a good clip, causing the last girl in the line to whip through the bend in the rink. The girl's free hand shot out to the side, hitting Marigold right in the shoulder. Not enough to really hurt, but enough to catch her off balance, and once again she was flapping her arms trying to stay upright as her feet slipped and tripped under her.

She was sure she was about to go ass over teakettle when, like some kind of wheeled superhero, Kasima was suddenly behind her, grabbing onto Marigold's hips to steady her. Her panic subsided and her feet stilled. She rolled along as if the moment had never happened. But Marigold doubted she would forget the way she felt with Kasima's remarkably strong arms supporting her. She felt safe. And happy. And before she even realized what was happening, a contented little sigh slipped out from between her lips.

Kasima's body went rigid behind her before putting some space between them and loosening her grasp. "Did I hurt you?" She'd apparently misinterpreted the sigh. "I'm sorry I grabbed you without asking. It was reflexive. I only meant to keep you from falling."

"Oh no. I didn't mind that," Marigold said, looking over her shoulder. She didn't mind that one bit. In fact, she wanted to close the gap between them once more, but instead Kasima rolled up beside her. For a moment Marigold was mesmerized by the way the lights danced across Kasima's ash-brown hair, making it shine with the bright colors. And then her feet got tangled up again, and she took several quick steps to regain her balance. With a sheepish grin, she hooked her arm through the elbow Kasima offered. "Maybe it would be best if I just held on to you."

Kasima met her gaze, but her easy smile faded as the upbeat music changed to a slow jam and the deejay announced it was time for a slow skate. "I'll get you safely to the other side of the rink. You don't have to couple skate with me."

The lead pit of disappointment settled in Marigold's belly. She didn't totally mind the sensation of hanging on to Kasima while they rolled along in time with the romantic strains of a love song. Her mind reeled to come up with an excuse to continue. "But I'm…I'm just getting my sea legs here. I'm literally on a roll."

She laughed at her own joke. Why was she acting like such a goof? She was an independent woman who went for what she wanted—why was she making excuses now? *Because this isn't a date, and this woman isn't really interested in you, she's just putting on a show for her family. A show you totally agreed to.* Still, when she'd agreed to that plan she'd had no idea how damned comforting it would feel to be supported by Kasima's strong arms. Nor did she have any idea how absolutely intoxicating the orange blossom scent that seemed to surround Kasima at all times was. It was like a creamsicle on steroids dipped in sex. So damned good. She should enjoy the moment while it lasted. "Besides, I really like…'Never Had a Dream Come True.' I haven't heard S Club 7 in forever. I used to love them."

Kasima's eyebrow quirked up as the smile returned to her beautiful face. Under the disco ball lights the sprinkle of freckles across the bridge of her nose were more noticeable than usual. They gave her a very girl-next-door vibe. "Me too."

"Then let's keep on skating."

* * *

Kasima grabbed two pieces of cake and joined Marigold at one of the small tables adjacent to the big one full of sugared-up eight-year-old revelers. With all the excited shrieks and loud laughter at the kids' table, deep conversation was unlikely, but she was glad to have just a little longer with Marigold before the party ended. "Let us eat cake." She hoped her half-smile would convey her awareness that it was a dorky joke. The grin she received in response confirmed it landed.

"I grabbed us each a water. I hope that's okay," Marigold said as she accepted one of the dinosaur-themed paper plates of cake. "There are pitchers of soda on the big table if you'd prefer it."

A glance over her shoulder confirmed the presence of various soft drinks—a choice her brother obviously thought was acceptable. "Who thought giving sugared-up kids caffeine was a good idea?" Kasima laughed. "There's only about thirty minutes left before the party ends. We'll be returning these kids to their parents at full voltage."

"Let the kids live it up." Marigold licked the fluffy buttercream from her fork. "There are few things in life like the joy of a birthday party when you're eight years old. I say they should enjoy that youthful jubilance while it lasts."

It was sweet of Marigold to put a positive spin on the sugar-fueled chaos around them. It was sweet of her to show up at the party at all. Certainly not part of their original deal. She'd basically been buffaloed into it by the family. Kasima's brain flip-flopped between whether she should feel embarrassed or grateful about that. She'd enjoyed her afternoon at the rink with Marigold and was disappointed that it was drawing to a close, but she couldn't impose on this kind woman any further. She'd played the part they'd originally agreed to and then some. Making any additional plans might give the impression that Kasima was looking for more, and that would be wrong. She was still firmly planted in the not-ready-to-date camp. "This is probably more youthful jubilance than you're used to, eh?"

"What, this?" Marigold gestured to indicate the scene around them. "This is nothing. I don't often work with clients this age, but I've worked with plenty of teenagers, and they can be much more chaotic. I've got one client now who—" She shook her head as if reconsidering the prudence of possibly oversharing proprietary work information. "Anyway, eight-year-old youthful jubilance is a pleasure compared to what teens are capable of, believe me."

The brief wariness that had flashed on Marigold's face indicated there was more to the story, but before Kasima could decide if she should push for it, they were interrupted by an excited Matty, still on wheels, who was obviously ready to get back to partying.

"Aunt Kas, don't leave, okay? We're going to play Skee-Ball, but I'll be back." A smear of green icing covered the corner of his grin, and Kasima gently wiped it away with her thumb.

"I won't go anywhere without you, but my friend Marigold might have to leave soon, so what do you say to her for coming to celebrate with you?"

"Thank you, Marigold," he replied dutifully before skating off.

"He's a sweet kid," Marigold commented as the rest of the partiers raced off after Matty. "He obviously adores you."

"I assure you, the feeling is mutual." She'd spent a lot of time with her dear nephew in the past few years. And he'd helped her as much as she'd helped him, but there was no need to get into that with Marigold when she was about to walk out of the party and, presumably, out of Kasima's life as well. The charade was nearly over. "He's my little buddy."

"I'm glad I got to meet him." Marigold pushed her chair back from the table and stood. "Thank you for inviting me today."

Kasima got up as well. This was it—time for them to part. At least she could walk her out. "Thanks for coming and for the gift. You really didn't have to do that."

"Are you kidding me? That was the most fun I've had shopping for a gift in forever. I can't remember the last time I went to a toy store."

As they reached the exit, Kasima considered how to say goodbye. After the way Marigold had clung to her when they were skating, a hug didn't seem inappropriate, but that clinging had been based on necessity. Their entire relationship was based on a lie. Would that kind of physical contact be acceptable now? She was relieved when Marigold made the decision for them and pulled her into a quick squeeze at the door.

"This weekend has been really fun," Marigold said, releasing her. "Thanks for getting me out of my rut. You don't know how much I needed it. And good luck with things at the brewery. Please thank your family and tell them…" She frowned. "Well, whatever. I'd say goodbye myself, but I just don't want to mislead them anymore, you know?"

"Oh yeah, no." Of course, Kasima understood. She'd been the one to escalate the whole situation with her family, not Marigold. Untangling this mess shouldn't be on her. "I'll handle that part. No worries."

"Great." The smile was back on Marigold's plump red lips. "See you around."

Kasima waved and Marigold slipped out the door. Their very brief, completely fake relationship was over. She returned to the party room and busied herself cleaning up the abandoned cake plates and half-empty cups of soda. It appeared Matty's party had been a success. So why did she feel like a party balloon that had lost its helium and sunk sadly to the floor?

She didn't want to get involved with anyone; she'd been certain of that. But she couldn't deny she'd enjoyed spending time with Marigold that weekend. They hadn't truly been dating. She knew that. Still, she felt a little sad that the whole thing was over.

Maybe the heavy feeling in her belly wasn't about Marigold at all. Maybe it was due to the fact that now she had to lie to her parents yet again, spinning them some sort of story about why she and Marigold were no longer seeing each other. She hadn't really thought that part through when she started this ruse, but after Marigold commented on not wanting to mislead them further, she realized that was really what they'd been doing in the first place. She didn't have to compound the lie this particular day and put a damper on the happy mood of Matty's birthday, but she would have to do it eventually. And soon.

"Aunt Kas!" Matty skated into the room and circled the table she was clearing. "Why are you in here by yourself?"

"I'm just cleaning up in here to help your mom and dad. They're busy being good hosts and talking to your friends' parents. I'm doing my part behind the scenes." That was the way she preferred it anyway. Her brother had always been the more sociable of the siblings. She was always perfectly content playing the supporting role. That was how they'd fallen into their roles in the family business—Spencer out front, a natural salesman, and her inside the brewery, following her passion and making the best product possible. "You should probably be out there too, thanking your friends for coming to your party. C'mon, I'll go with you."

"Don't forget your sunglasses." Matty pointed at the table she'd been sitting at while eating cake.

"I didn't wear sunglasses—" But when she glanced at the table she recognized the glasses right away. "Those are Marigold's. I'll make sure she gets them back. Thanks, Matty."

Marigold had left her sunglasses behind. Her Prada sunglasses—no doubt expensive ones. They would have to be returned, and that meant Kasima would get to—*have to*—see her again. The deflated party balloon in her chest had been suddenly buoyed by a second wind. She would text Marigold and let her know she had the sunglasses, and they could make arrangements to meet up and hand them off. Just one more meeting—strictly functional—to return the forgotten item. And then they would be done.

CHAPTER SEVEN

Monday morning Marigold sat at her sleek glass-and-chrome desk in her office overlooking the city and stared at the text message from Kasima. After spending Sunday afternoon at the roller rink, she'd gone home determined to catch up on the work emails and the phone calls she'd neglected all weekend. She'd ended up spending a lot of the afternoon thinking about all the fun she'd had at the party. Skating to the upbeat music, playing air hockey, laughing at stupid jokes, and hanging out with a pretty woman. It was hard to reconcile that good time with the fact that the ruse was over and they wouldn't be spending any more time together. It was probably best if she tried harder not to reflect on it. That's why, when Kasima's text had popped up Sunday evening, Marigold had put off responding to it. But now her silence was stretching into the territory of being rude. She needed to say *something*.

Yes, she wanted her sunglasses back, and it was certainly generous of Kasima to offer to deliver them, but it was the whole meeting up again part that had her dragging her feet on sending a response. It wasn't that she didn't want to see Kasima again—it was exactly the opposite of that. She very much *did* want to see Kasima again. Each time they had hung out she'd learned things about her that drew her in. Like the way Kasima and her family worked with the conservation group to give some balance back to the ecosystem where the brewery operated. Or the sweet way Kasima interacted with her nephew.

But their arrangement had been clear from the very start—they were only pretending to date for the fundraiser. And then for the skating party. But that was it. Kasima wasn't interested in dating her for real for whatever reason, and Marigold didn't have time to be a good girlfriend anyway. Shutting down any feelings that may be blossoming was the only way to handle this, and if avoidance made it easier, then so be it. The Prada glasses might just have to be collateral damage.

Before she could ponder the topic any further, Georgette the receptionist buzzed in from her desk in the lobby. "Ms. Luxe, your nine o'clock is here."

A second voice came through the speaker. "She knows who I am. Ava Ashford. You can just say my name. Say it."

"You certainly do not have to say her name, Georgette." Marigold sighed. This kid was too much. "But please do send her in."

Marigold set her phone screen-side down on her desk so she wouldn't be tempted to read Kasima's message for the millionth time. She turned her attention back to the numerous open tabs on her computer screens. Articles and listicles containing mention of Ava Ashford's recent hotel hijinks. Where her full focus should have been all morning instead of rereading a text from a woman who didn't want to date her. Marigold had managed to get the trashed hotel room story under control for the most part, but now it was time for Ava to make some public appearances and show that she was back on track. Getting that under control—specifically keeping Ava on message—might be a whole other story.

"Have you seen what they're saying about me on the Internet?" Ava whined as she strode into the office. No niceties. Right to it.

"I've pulled up a few sites." Marigold turned one of her monitors so it could be seen from the opposite side of the desk, where Ava had dropped dramatically into the leopard-print upholstered chair.

"There hasn't been a new story about what happened in that hotel in over two days."

"You're welcome."

"That's not a good thing," Ava scoffed with a toss of her blond curls. "You know what they say, any publicity is good publicity. No one is talking about me."

Typical Ava Ashford behavior—expecting nothing less than "all eyes on me." Marigold had become accustomed to it over the past few months, although recently it had seemed to have ratcheted up a few notches. Ava never acted this way before she got the part of Dakota Oakley, that was for sure.

Prior to this role, though Ava had been a client of the agency, a child actor getting commercials, walk-ons, and bit parts, Marigold hadn't been her agent. Marigold had only been assigned to her once this larger-than-life ego developed. The basic premise of *Homestead Hollow* was a small community trying to survive in an apocalyptic Wild West. It was very niche and fairly queer, and from the time the promotional tour began, folks had latched onto Ava's character—the sapphic in the ensemble. Apparently, that was all it took to launch Ava's ego into the stratosphere. And as the first season of the show went on, captured a more mainstream audience, and secured renewal for a second season, Ava's self-importance had continued to grow. As had Marigold's headaches when it came to managing her career.

Working with Ava wasn't the first time Marigold had been assigned one of the McClancy-Jansen Agency's difficult clients. She was known as the fixer around the office, and she was good at what she did. Still, it didn't make working with those particular clients any less exhausting. Ava was no exception.

Marigold suspected Ava's declaration that "any publicity was good publicity" was merely an excuse for her bad behavior. That old adage may have held true back in the day, but it was definitely an antiquated notion. Marigold knew better than that, and she also wasn't buying into the line of bull Ava was selling. She frowned at the young woman across her desk.

"That sentiment no longer holds true in this digital age. Your publicity should be handled with much more finesse and purposefulness. We've done some damage control, which I believe is why you're seeing a dip in online scuttlebutt about the story, but you're still going to have to face the media directly about it at some point."

Ava opened her mouth as if she was ready to argue, but Marigold didn't give her a chance. She held up a hand to stop her and pushed on with her message. "To that end, I've booked you on the late-night television circuit. You'll be asked about the incident, and you're going to work with a tightly scripted response."

"A scripted response? Nuh-uh." Ava crossed her arms and shook her head like a petulant child. If her feet had been on the floor instead of propped over the arm of the chair she was sitting on, Marigold imagined Ava would be stomping them. "No script. I do what I like. That's my whole brand."

It was a brand that Marigold was one hundred percent on a mission to modify. "Not this time. You're simply going to explain that you invited some people back to your hotel room and unfortunately things got out of control. You regret that you made that decision, and you adamantly do not condone the type of property damage that resulted. You're sorry that you made the choice to invite the group to your room."

"So, I'm going to shift blame to my friends?"

"You and I both know those people were not your friends. They were an ad hoc entourage you picked up over the course of your night, lured in with tequila shots and God only knows what else." Marigold cringed inwardly, remembering the state of that hotel room as well as the condition of the stragglers she'd chased out of there when she'd gone to retrieve Ava. "Honestly, I don't even want to know what else. Regardless, your statement will not be entirely untrue. Plus you'll be showing remorse as you apologize for your poor choices."

Ava's hand-painted Vans slammed to the floor as she finally sat properly in the chair. At least she was paying attention. "Those people wanted to hang out with me because I'm a big freaking deal. I can't say that shit and be all remorseful." Her downturned lips made it clear how distasteful she found the word. "I have a reputation to maintain."

"You being a 'big freaking deal' will be very short-lived if you don't clean up that reputation." She heard Allison's voice in her head—"kid-glove treatment"—and knew she should bite her tongue, but she was losing patience with her client and the conversation. "There are thousands of young women out there who can do what you do on camera—despite what you may think, you can be replaced. You need to give people a reason to want to work with you, and a dose of humility could go a long way toward that. Otherwise, this good thing will be over before you know it."

Marigold knew that feeling all too well after her weekend with Kasima. Even though it had started out as a brief distraction from dealing with her job and Ava's big, bad, ego energy, by the time she was leaving the skating rink she'd felt their time together had been much too short. It was a shame that the whole thing had been nothing more than a ruse. She'd enjoyed spending time with Kasima. Maybe she should take her own advice and hold on to the good thing while she could. Perhaps one more get-together just to have some coffee and retrieve her sunglasses wouldn't be such a bad idea.

"So, there's a script for what I'm going to say?" Ava had sunk down a bit in her chair. It seemed like something Marigold said to her had gotten through.

Marigold nodded. "Just let me send one quick text and we'll go over it."

CHAPTER EIGHT

Kasima was already enjoying a piping-hot cup of coffee when Marigold walked into the cafe and signaled she was going to grab a drink before sitting down. The Prada sunglasses were set on the table waiting for their owner. This meeting was strictly business, Kasima kept reminding herself.

She glanced over at Marigold, who looked stunning and yet also very business savvy in a tailored cream suit. The pale neutral was a striking contrast to her dark auburn hair. The overall effect was classic beauty. She looked good. Really good. As if sensing she was being studied, Marigold looked back at the table. Kasima had been caught staring. Marigold flashed a bright smile that made her forest-green eyes sparkle. Kasima managed a polite half-smile before breaking eye contact under the guise of taking a sip of coffee.

Something about that exchange didn't feel strictly business at all. Perhaps she should have just sent the sunglasses to Marigold's office by Taskrabbit or something and avoided this reunion. Everything would be fine. She didn't have to drag their meeting out. She would hand off the glasses, finish her coffee, and go on her way. She wouldn't lead this kind, beautiful woman on.

Marigold slid into the chair across the table and set her mug down. "This blonde vanilla latte smells divine. I can't wait to suck it down as soon as it cools a pinch." She seemed to catch Kasima's questioning look. "I'm sorry, I know I sound ridiculous. I think they're delicious, but they're so calorie-laden I only have them every once in a while. Like a special treat. Anyway, what are you drinking?"

Kasima's gaze dropped to her mug and its boring contents. "Just black coffee for me. It's the only way I drink it." No special treat for her, just caffeine.

"Au naturale." Marigold nodded. "That suits you."

Now that they were face-to-face, Kasima could see the olive-green camisole under Marigold's jacket and the delicate beading on the neckline that dipped down just enough to reveal a hint of cleavage. Kasima shook her head to clear it of the thoughts that conjured up. She shouldn't be eying up this woman's body; she should do the thing she was there to do.

"Here are your sunglasses. You should put them in your bag now so you don't forget them again."

"Right," Marigold said, tucking them into her buttery leather Kate Spade purse. "Thanks again for finding them."

"It was actually Matty who spotted them," she confessed.

"That kid. I knew he was a good one. I appreciate you meeting me to return them. And it's…nice to see you again."

Kasima liked the way Marigold's smile sweetened when she spoke of Matty. "My pleasure. I mean, it was no problem." *My pleasure? What the hell?*

Luckily before the moment had the chance to dial up to completely awkward, Kasima's phone rang.

"Go ahead and get that if you need to," Marigold said between sips of still-steaming blonde vanilla latte. "I understand that sometimes work calls can't wait."

"I hardly ever get work calls." She glanced at the phone screen. *Of course.* She'd mentioned to her dad that she was meeting Marigold for coffee before coming into work. He was probably just happy for his daughter's reentry to the dating world after years of self-imposed solitude. But what if there was some kind of emergency situation at the brewery that she needed to be aware of? Like a disastrous incident with those old fermentation tanks? "But it's my dad, so I'm just going to pick up real quick."

* * *

Marigold tried not to eavesdrop on Kasima's phone call, but they were sitting at the same small cafe table. How could she not overhear what was being said? She focused on the delicious toasty vanilla goodness of her latte. It was one of the most comforting flavors—like a warm hug for her tastebuds. It was just so… "Mmmm."

She hadn't realized the moan was out loud until Kasima shot a wide-eyed look her way.

"Sorry!" Marigold whispered with an apologetic wave, trying to disappear behind her big, colorful mug. It didn't stop her from hearing Kasima's side of the conversation though.

"I'm not going to ask her now. I'll ask her later," Kasima said into the phone with a strained tone. "Well, yes, we are, but—"

Marigold peeked out from behind the mug. Well, that was curious. Was Kasima talking about her?

"Fine," Kasima said before blowing out a sigh of surrender and looking at Marigold. "My dad wants to know when you're coming by the brewery to help me with the special brew."

She remembered the topic coming up on Friday night at the fundraiser, but she had been certain Kasima would shut it down since their agreement had only covered that first fake date. That was before the whole skating party thing, which was technically a second fake date. Still, there was no reason for her to make yet another appearance, especially at the family business.

"Me? Helping you at the brewery?" she said softly, pointing at herself.

Kasima nodded slowly. Into the phone she said, "I know she told you she's a beer lover. That's true. Yes, she's very excited about it. She's actually speechless."

"Not so much speechless as wondering why your dad thinks you and I are working on the special brew together. How does he know we're even—"

Kasima held up a hand to silence her. "Okay, Dad, we'll work out the details and get back to you. Gotta run. Bye."

Kasima set her phone on the table and went back to drinking her black coffee as if nothing had happened, but Marigold couldn't ignore the fact that Mr. Powell had been on the other end of that call talking about her.

"What was that about?"

"That was my dad."

That was it? That was *all* she was going to say?

"I know it was your dad." Marigold's words were clipped as she struggled not to raise her voice in the quiet little cafe. "What I meant was, how did he know we were having coffee together today?"

"Because he thinks we are on a date."

"You told him we were on a date? Why would you do that?"

Now it was Kasima's turn to try to hide behind her mug. "Because I told him you're my girlfriend." She hurried on before Marigold could respond. "But I didn't mean to mislead him. He was just so excited that I was bringing a date to the fundraiser, and he looked so happy that I wasn't all sad and alone, and then at some point he referred to you as my girlfriend, and I didn't correct him. It sort of snowballed from there. I'm sorry. I never meant to drag you into it."

Marigold inhaled a deep breath of coffee bean-infused air. There was a lot to digest in the words that had just poured out of Kasima, and she definitely had some follow-up questions, but first things first.

"You told your family I'm your girlfriend?"

Kasima gave a pitiful shrug. Her beautiful wide brown eyes made it impossible for Marigold to really be mad at her. "I guess I didn't think about the part where I'd have to tell them we broke up. It's going to be especially hard to tell my dad. He really took a liking to you."

"And I like him too," Marigold said, and she meant it. Brian had been kind to her from the moment they had met. Even now—he was following up on her coming by the brewery because he remembered she said she was a beer lover. That was so thoughtful.

But, come on…girlfriend? She couldn't be part of keeping this lie alive. Pretending to be someone she wasn't was behavior she had left firmly in her past—career-wise and in her personal life too. Even if Kasima's family gave her a warm and fuzzy feeling that she wasn't ready to let go. And even if Kasima herself was super cool, a lot of fun to hang around with, and pretty damn easy on the eyes as well. None of that mattered, because this thing between Kasima and her—it was nothing more than a lie. And it would be cruel to repay the kindness this family had shown her with deceit. No matter how much she loved beer and enjoyed spending time with their daughter.

"I do like him," she repeated. "Which is why I don't want to lie to him. We definitely are not girlfriends. We're not even really dating, right? I mean, this isn't truly a date. We only met so you could return my sunglasses. None of the times we've hung out were real dates, were they?"

Kasima's hesitation made Marigold's pulse race. Was she going to say it wasn't totally a lie to her? Was she curious if there was something genuine between them as well?

Kasima took a gulp of coffee, licked her lips, and glanced down at her hands before meeting Marigold's gaze again. "No. You're right." That was that. "But I really could use another opinion to help me decide on which beer to brew for the special release, and since you're a beer drinker, you'd be the perfect person to assist. I could even give you a tour of the brewery."

She sighed as if the next thing she had to say wasn't as chipper of a topic as beer tasting. "And it would help me to let them all down easy. I mean, I know I need to tell my family the truth about us, but my dad is so excited about showing you the brewery. We could just do this one last thing together. You know, for him."

"For him," Marigold echoed, testing the idea. She really wouldn't mind the chance to check out the brewery—she was all for supporting local businesses. Plus, Kasima seemed to think her dad really wanted her to be involved in choosing the beer for the special brew. It sure didn't seem like Kasima was interested in anything more than just letting her family down easy, so that would be the end of it for sure this time. No more pretending to be a couple. No more lying to her family. "Of course. But then that's it for you and me and this girlfriends thing. You'll set everyone straight?"

"Definitely. That's it for the girlfriends thing. I'll ease him into the fact that we're not together."

"We're not together," Marigold echoed. Kasima's message was crystal clear. "But we will taste some beer for the sake of SoCal Wildlife Rescue."

"And you'll get a tour as well." Kasima smiled and her eyes flashed brightly. But it was probably just the anticipation of a trip to the brewery that made Marigold's chest buzz with excitement.

CHAPTER NINE

On her way home from work, Marigold made a pit stop for dinner with her best friend. She gave a quick knock on the back door of Elle and Ashley's house but didn't wait for a response before entering. She was immediately met by the warm, rich aroma of tomato sauce and yeasty dough. Her best friend's house was one of her favorite places on Earth, both for the company there and the food. She found Elle and her teenage daughter, Luci, in the kitchen. "Mmmm. Is it pasta night?"

"Pizza. Ashley had a dinner meeting with the folks from the Eats! Channel, so I let Luci select the meal." Elle held up the log of mozzarella she was slicing, but the food prep didn't stop her from getting in a teasing jab at her best friend. "Glad to see you're working on your work-life balance. It's great to see you outside of your office before seven o'clock."

"Don't get too excited." Marigold sighed. "This is technically business-related since I'm dropping off these papers from the Eats! Channel for you to sign." She placed a manila folder on the counter. "I know how you like your paper trail. You should use

Docusign or something. You're killing trees. Back me up on this, Luci."

"Ugh. Business talk." The teenager rolled her eyes. "You're on your own, Aunt Mari. Text me when the pizza is ready, Mom."

"I'm not going to text," Elle called after her daughter as she left the kitchen. "I'm just going to yell like moms have been doing since the beginning of time."

Marigold waited until she was sure Luci was out of earshot before continuing, "Anyway, I've got miles to go before I sleep tonight. After dinner I'm headed straight home to work on spinning all this Ava Ashford crap."

"She's still refusing to play nice?" Elle moved on to grating a block of Parmesan. "Haven't you been able to work your Marigold Luxe magic on her?"

Marigold hitched her hip onto one of the stools on the side of the island counter opposite from where Elle was working. "I managed to get her to agree to a scripted response for the late-night circuit, but she's such a wild card. She could go rogue at any moment. Who knows what she'll actually say once her ego is bolstered by the spotlight. I'll be holding my breath until the last set goes dark."

She shifted on the stool and rested the heels of her Italian leather oxfords on the bottom rung. There were few places more comforting to hang out in than Elle's kitchen, and she was settling in for a bit. It had been a hell of a day between dealing with Ava and then the whole meeting with Kasima.

Kasima's family had actually thought they were girlfriends? That was a far throw from what she had agreed to. And now she was locked into one more get-together with Kasima. She didn't really mind the hanging-out-with-Kasima part, but it was the whole girlfriends' charade she could do without. It was hard to not consider these activities as dates at this point. Fancy dinners, roller-skating, beer tasting—all classic date fodder. Which was why she was trying her damnedest not to think about it at all. Instead, she would do what she did best—bury herself in her work.

"I just don't get why these difficult clients always seem to get transferred to my roster," Marigold sighed. "Some days I feel like

I'm nothing more than a glorified babysitter. Remember Jack Belvey? Ugh. Or Jade Michelina? Why she thought wearing a Burmese python to walk the red carpet at the Emmy Awards was a good idea, I'll never understand. What a disaster."

"Hey, only three paparazzi were bit by that snake, and they all lived to tell." Elle smirked. "Besides, you turned Jade and the other clients around, and you'll do the same with Ava Ashford. McClancy-Jansen gives you these clients because they know you can handle them. You have a gift. Hey, do you think that's why you're my agent—because I'm a problem client?"

"Ha, ha." Marigold pinched a cherry tomato from the salad bowl and popped it into her mouth. She was starving. After interrupting her workday to meet Kasima for coffee, she'd decided to work through lunch. All she'd had to eat since then was a thumbprint cookie out of a cheery pink bakery box someone had left in the office break room. "No way. I handpicked you as a client. Though, God knows, you've had your moments too."

"Fair point." Elle gave a snort of laughter as she finished assembling the pizzas. The two of them had been doing this comfortable back-and-forth since they were teenagers. That was also the reason why Elle could read her so well. "Are you sure the Ava Ashford situation is the only thing on your mind? You're doing that weird thing with your tongue that you do when something is really bugging you."

Marigold hadn't even realized she was running her tongue across her teeth, but she abruptly stopped. "There's nothing bugging—"

"I'm gonna stop you right there," Elle interrupted her. "There's obviously something eating at you, and I'm guessing it's something about the sexy brewmaster you've been hanging around with. Now, you can tell me it's nothing and bite back your little secrets and feelings, but that will only force me to make up my own version of what is transpiring. And I think we both know that I have a heck of an imagination. Or you could just nip this whole thing in the bud and tell me what's going on with you."

"I'm not…She's not a…" Marigold sputtered to a stop. Knowing her best friend, she wouldn't let the subject go until she got the scoop. There was no use trying to sidestep it; Elle was onto her. "It's about the sexy brewmaster I've been hanging around with," she admitted before relaying the whole tale of how the fake date at the fundraiser turned into a second get-together at a roller rink, which led to their coffee meeting earlier that day.

"She told her family you're her girlfriend when you're not even dating?" Elle cringed. "That feels a little red-flaggy."

"No, it wasn't like that." Marigold shook her head and carried the salad to the kitchen table to give herself a moment to think. Kasima had only told her dad they were involved to keep him from worrying about her. What was it she'd said? Because he looked so happy that she wasn't sad and alone. That wasn't red-flaggy. That was being a considerate daughter. "She was just trying to please a parent. Who among us doesn't know that feeling?"

Elle shot her a pointed look.

"Okay," Marigold acquiesced. "Parent pleasing was never exactly *my* strong suit, but still, I get it. We told one little lie about going on a date and it snowballed. You know how I feel about pretending to be something I'm not. I won't keep this up. After we do the beer tasting at the brewery, that will be the end of it. We will officially no longer be fake dating. We will be fake broken up."

"Hold up." Elle had been combining ingredients for the salad dressing but stopped midshake to gape at her. "You're having *another* date with Kasima? What's that, your fourth now?"

"Nuh-uh. No. It's definitely not a date this time. I'm just going over to taste test some new products they're brewing because her dad remembered I'm a beer lover and he asked me to help Kasima select one to brew for this special thing they're doing. And that man is so kind and sweet—I understand how Kasima feels. I don't want to disappoint him either. So, I agreed to go."

Elle frowned. "You're telling me you've attended a formal fundraiser with this woman, gone to a family function with her, met for coffee just this morning, and now plan to help her with some special project that her family is involved with? You are not fake dating Kasima. You are *actually* dating Kasima."

Marigold helped herself to a glass of wine. Suddenly her mouth was desperately dry. "Don't say that. Please." A large gulp of merlot emboldened her to spill the truth that had been simmering under the surface for her all day. "I'm really starting to like Kasima. She's fun and smart, and God, she's gorgeous. But she's made it clear again and again that she doesn't want a relationship—she doesn't even want to date. That's how we got into this whole mess in the first place. She told her folks we were together just to get them off her back for not wanting to date anyone. So, I have to put my guard up and not let my feelings grow. Because there's no sense in setting myself up for a fall."

Elle's eyes were full of pity as she filled her own glass with wine. "You're not even going to give it a try? Just tell her how you feel. See what happens from there."

"Hell no. I feel stupid enough that I've started to develop feelings for her. We had an agreement. I knew what this was from the start." She didn't care how many times Elle blinked those big puppy dog eyes at her, she was standing strong on this. "We'll do the taste test together as friends, but that's it. I'm out."

"You're out?"

"I'm out," she repeated. It would become a mantra if that's what it took. A daily affirmation. She could have T-shirts made. "I have my hands full with the Ava Ashford situation anyway. I need to focus on work."

"Okay, sure. Work." Elle gave her a doubtful grimace. "Let me know how that works out for you."

"Works out for me? I get it. You're very funny."

"And I'm very hungry." Elle gave her shoulder a squeeze. "Come on, let's eat before you have to get back to Ava Ashford land."

CHAPTER TEN

Later that week, possibly encouraged by Elle's reminder that she remained lacking in the parent-pleasing department, Marigold went to the assisted-living home where her mother, Constance, resided. She usually visited a couple of times a week, but since she'd spent the previous weekend with Kasima, it had been almost a full week since she'd been there. Constance probably didn't notice, but it still caused a pang of guilt in Marigold's gut. She needed to keep up their visitation schedule no matter what else popped up in her life. She owed Constance that much.

As she stepped into the dark wood-paneled room of the common space, she spotted Constance bent over her favorite table in the far corner intently working on a jigsaw puzzle, oblivious to the other residents, who were either watching television or shuffling around the room socializing. Constance Luxe did not seem to care that she'd made zero friends in the nearly three years she'd been residing at Juniper Hills Assisted Living Home. As far as Marigold could tell, she preferred solitude to mingling with the others. At least that had been the case most days since she'd been living there.

This was a change from Marigold's childhood, where Constance would speak to anyone and everyone who got in her way or just happened to be within earshot. Back then her favorite topic of conversation was her daughter, rising child star. But then that star's trajectory changed, or at least it wasn't a trajectory they followed together any longer, and that particular thread of conversation had been abandoned.

"Hello, Connie." Marigold's voice was higher than usual, even to her own ear, but she was determined to keep the tone of her visit cheerful. "How are you today?"

"I'm fine, I suppose." Constance didn't look up from the project in front of her. Her affinity for jigsaw puzzles was relatively new as well—Marigold had never witnessed her working on one until she relocated to Juniper Hills. Was this an activity she had taken up when she'd moved from California to Missouri, where she'd lived with her second husband? Whom Marigold had never actually met? Who was to say? That was the sort of information Constance no longer divulged. "They served split pea soup with lunch today, and I abhor split pea soup."

"I'm sure tomorrow's soup will be something more tolerable." Marigold slipped her blazer off and folded it neatly over the back of the chair before she sat. Her mother would probably have something to say about her untoned middle-aged shoulders and upper arms being bare in public, but she'd risk it. They kept the thermostat set at slightly north of balmy at Juniper Hills. It was either bare shoulders or pit stains. Bare shoulders won every time. "Anything else happening here today?"

She'd learned over the past couple of years that their visits went best when she began first thing with somewhat vague questions to gauge her mother's mood and lucidity.

Constance suddenly looked up from the puzzle and met her gaze. "Marigold, what are you doing here? You're supposed to be at your audition. You can't just waltz into these things whenever you please. No one wants to work with a diva." She shook an angry finger to emphasize her point.

"I retired from acting almost twenty years ago, remember? I'm on the other side of things now—an agent trying to wrangle the divas."

Constance's forehead crinkled in confusion, but before she had a chance to respond, the women were joined by one of the caregivers at the home. Susan's constantly wide eyes and overly bright smile always made it seem like she'd just had one too many espresso shots. But she was friendly, and Marigold appreciated the attention and good care she gave Constance.

"Hello, Miss Marigold. Come to work on a puzzle with your mother today?"

In all the times she'd visited Juniper Hills, Marigold had never helped with a puzzle—Constance wouldn't allow it. She also hadn't called Constance Mother or Mom or anything other than her first name since she was eight years old. Another of Constance's staunch decrees. "Connie" was as casual as it got.

"I think she's doing just fine on her own. I just came by to find out why you keep trying to feed her split pea soup." She winked at Susan.

"Miss Connie hates split pea soup, I know. Her feelings about it are not a secret."

"Very funny, you two. I'm sitting right here and there's nothing wrong with my hearing." Constance paused her puzzling to scold them. "Talking about me right in front of my face is plain rude."

"We're just teasing, honey, but you're right and I apologize," Susan said and patted Marigold on the shoulder. She might look perpetually excited, but she had a very calming effect on the residents. "I'll let you get back to your visit. Let me know if you need anything."

When it was just the two of them again, Marigold returned to her assessment. "Would you believe I went roller-skating last week?"

"Roller-skating?" Constance actually laughed. She seemed to be connected with the here and now again, and Marigold blew out a breath of relief. "Whatever possessed you to do that?"

"It was a friend's nephew's birthday party."

Marigold didn't bother to add that her interest in Kasima felt more than just friendly. There was no reason to bring up a subject that was a moot point. "It was fun, but for days I had aches in muscles I'd forgotten I even had."

"You always wanted to go skating when you were a child. I never understood why you wanted to partake in risky behavior. You were some kind of thrill seeker."

The response was another good sign. Marigold pulled a scrapbook from her tote bag. It was part of a collection of photos and ephemera she had gathered to help spark—or maybe hold on to—Constance's memory. The assortment was one of many tips she'd gleaned from the Internet for working with a loved one who'd experienced a brain injury.

She placed the book on the corner of the table, careful not to disturb the puzzle, and opened it to a page filled with reminders of family celebrations from Marigold's childhood, meant to launch the two of them on a trip down memory lane. Some days it worked, other times Constance couldn't be bothered to drag her attention away from the puzzle she was working on. Which one Marigold would get, she never knew, but either way, she had to try. She hadn't been a known parent-pleaser in the past, but at least she could try to make up for it now. Maybe then she could deal with the guilt she lived with for what she'd done.

CHAPTER ELEVEN

Kasima sat at one of the tables by the big store front window in the taproom and picked at a hangnail on her left middle finger. She couldn't help it; she was nervous about this meeting with Marigold.

Because the Enchanted Hops Brewing Company campus could be hard to navigate if you weren't accustomed to the layout of the buildings, she had arranged to meet Marigold in the taproom and begin their tour there. She'd given plenty of private tours of the brewery before—that wasn't the root cause of her nerves. It was more the Marigold factor of this particular private tour.

Although she'd ultimately agreed to it, it was clear to Kasima that there had definitely been some reluctance on Marigold's part when she was invited to the brewery. She was guessing it wasn't all about misleading her family. In fairness, Kasima wasn't one hundred percent sold on hanging out with Marigold either. Their date at the fundraiser was meant to be a one-time thing. Then her family had roped Marigold into the skating party. Now this tour. The whole one-fake-date-to-appease-her-parents thing had swung wildly out of control. But the only alternative she could see to not going through with the tour once her father had extended the offer was to tell him that taking Marigold to the fundraiser had been a ruse in the first place. Which meant facing her parents' disappointed expressions and perhaps their anger that she'd lied to them. So she'd agreed to give a tour and put that unpleasantness off for just a teensy bit longer. She was still going to have to fabricate a whole breakup story, yet another lie. She didn't like it, but it was her own fault. And anyway, it was almost over.

Luckily, before she could sink any further into her guilt over lying to her family, Marigold walked through the taproom door. Despite her nerves, Kasima's chest suddenly felt lighter when their gazes met. Marigold seemed to have that effect on her every time they met. She was dressed in faded blue jeans with a few strategically placed rips in them, a black-and-white-striped long-sleeved T-shirt, and bright orange Adidas sneakers that added the perfect pop of color to the ensemble. God, the woman had style.

"Welcome to Enchanted Hops. I thought you were coming here straight from work," Kasima said, giving her outfit another once-over—this time more obvious—as she stood to greet her properly. "Is your firm big on casual Thursdays or something?"

"You told me to wear comfortable footwear and that this would be a hands-on tour." Marigold's bright smile revealed her perfect teeth—a Hollywood smile. The kind that lit up a space. "I took you at your word."

"I'm glad. A lot of people don't, and then we have to skip certain parts of the brewery because they're wearing open-toed shoes or something."

Marigold had actually listened to her and taken her advice. That was nice. There was nothing worse than giving instruction only for someone to completely ignore you because they were certain they knew better or that your rules were arbitrary.

"Want anything to drink before we get started?" Kasima gestured to the bar.

Marigold arched a curious eyebrow. "Isn't that what we're here to do? Drink beer?"

"My dad is going to meet us in the test kitchen. I figured on the way I could give you the tour. Then we'll get to the testing," Kasima promised.

They stepped outside and Kasima squinted against the setting sun. The days were getting longer now that it was April. It was still plenty light out as they crossed the campus from taproom to brew house.

"You have a lot of space here," Marigold said, gesturing to the buildings around them. "I didn't expect all this."

Many people liked beer. Few people gave much thought into how it gets into their frosty mug, so she took the comment in stride. "We brew a lot of beer and that takes a lot of space. I'm curious. What were you expecting?"

Marigold laughed her rich, sexy laugh. "I guess I didn't know."

"We handle the complete process here. From brewing to canning. And the taproom too, of course. But we'll start the tour at the beginning." Kasima held the brewery door open for her. "This is where it all starts—at the grain mill."

"This becomes beer?" Marigold peered suspiciously over the edge of the nearest hopper and at the barley it held.

Kasima nodded. "The mill crushes the malted barley and exposes the sugar inside it. Then we add hot water and let it do its thing for a bit." She led Marigold past the mash tuns. "When the wort—the liquid that's going to end up as beer—goes into these tanks over here, it will boil for a couple of hours. This is where we add the hops."

"There's a word I recognize." Marigold's triumphant gaze scanned the row of stainless steel tanks. She held up a finger. "I knew there were hops in beer."

"Did you know hops are flowers?" Kasima assumed from Marigold's raised eyebrows that she did not. "It's true. The type of hops we use and how much we add determines the flavor of the brew. It can be bitter or aromatic—it all happens here." She stopped short when she realized Marigold was studying her intently. "What is it?"

"It's just…you." She flashed that light-up-the-room smile again. It was the kind of smile that made you feel like you were in the company of an old friend—warm, comfortable, valued. "The way you're talking about the process and these steel tanks and grains. Your passion for the process and your family business is evident. It's a good look on you."

Heat burned at the top of Kasima's ears. It was surely just because she didn't expect a compliment from Marigold and not because she cared that Marigold thought she looked good. "Does that mean you want to see more?"

"I really do." Marigold nodded. "What happens after you add the hops?"

"The beer goes into the whirlpool."

"That sounds fun." She wiggled her eyebrows suggestively.

Kasima laughed. "It's science. The liquid is pumped in a circular motion around the tank, forcing the solids into the middle so they don't get sucked up with the beer when it's transferred out of the vessel. After that it has to cool, then it's on to the fermentation tank, but those tanks are kept in a whole other building."

"Hey! Fermentation! That's another thing I already knew about beer."

"It's a very important part of the process. Ales are fermented at a warmer temperature, lagers at a cooler one."

Marigold seemed to think about that. "I never really thought of making beer as science, but it totally is. You're a scientist."

"I really am." Kasima shrugged. "I've got the credentials to prove it too. I was a chemistry major in college."

"That's very cool." Marigold's gaze held hers, pupils wide.

Kasima felt a tug in her middle somewhere behind her belly button. It was time to wrap up the tour and get back to business. "We should probably get to the beer-tasting portion of the evening, since that's what you came here for, after all."

"Yeah." A slight cringe flickered across Marigold's expression. "I'd like to make it clear that although I'm definitely looking forward to the beer, I had no idea how much I would enjoy the tour. I think that's largely due to my tour guide. Thank you for taking the time to show me how beer is made."

The heat ratcheted up a notch, and Kasima couldn't stop the smile that split her face. There was no denying she was charmed.

"It was totally my pleasure to share my passion with you." Why did she say that? She was acting so awkward. Her mind raced to course correct. *And say something like a normal person.* "So, want some beer?"

* * *

Marigold followed Kasima past even more ginormous tanks on their way to their next destination. Had she overstepped on their agreement by complimenting her? She had meant what she said, so why not let it be known? But Kasima had ended the tour rather abruptly.

It wasn't that Marigold hadn't been interested in the tour of the brewery before she had arrived at Enchanted Hops—she really did appreciate the chance to learn how her favorite beverage was made. But she didn't expect that it would be just the two of them strolling around the brewery that day. She had been under the impression that this would be more of a group project—or at least include Brian, since he was the one who had actually invited her out to the brewery. The more time she spent one-on-one with Kasima, the harder it was to understand why there was no potential for anything romantic between the two of them. Was she wrong about the vibes she'd been getting whenever they hung out? Besides, technically the rules they'd put in place had only applied to the fundraiser outing. They'd never renegotiated the terms. Was she supposed to still follow them? Or were they null and void now that the two of them were more like actual friends?

Thankfully, when they entered a smaller room Kasima called the "test kitchen" near the back of the building, there was Brian, standing behind a bar washing glassware and humming along to the Foo Fighters song playing on the radio.

"Hey, Marigold, nice to see you again, dear. Come on in and have a seat." He gestured at the stools across the bar from him.

The term of endearment warmed her heart. She wasn't used to having a dad figure in her life. It was nice. Marigold thanked him and looped the straps of her bag over the high back of the tall stool before climbing onto it. This room was like a mix of the spaces she'd seen at the brewery thus far. Like the taproom, it had a bar, glassware, and a sleek, black steel glass-front back bar cooler full of cans of beer, but instead of the cozy decor of that space, the walls of the test kitchen had the same sterile, industrial aesthetic as the rest of the brewery building with its concrete block and exposed steel beams.

"We've completed a brief tour of the brewery," Kasima said with a pointed look in her direction. "And I believe Marigold is ready to get to the tasting portion of her visit."

"I don't blame you." Brian's smile was warm as he lined up glassware on the bar. "The tasting is definitely the best part."

It was remarkable how comfortable Marigold felt in the presence of these folks she had basically just met. Every time she'd crossed paths with Brian he'd made it a point to let her know she was welcome and included her in whatever the family was doing. "What do you have for us today?"

"Kasima, since you're the brewer, why don't you do the talking. I'll do the pouring." Brian held up a full growler of beer to emphasize his point.

The first option was an intimidatingly dark-brown beer topped with a thin layer of creamy foam. "This is a porter," Kasima explained. "But I've given it a little something extra. Tell me what you taste."

Marigold pulled the glass towards her. It wasn't a full tumbler-sized glass. It held maybe four or five ounces—the kind of glassware that would be used to serve a flight of beer. "I've never had a porter before. It's so dark." She inhaled the aroma and was struck by a note of chocolate.

"You drink coffee, right?" Brian grabbed his glass as she nodded. "You can handle a porter. It's the same kind of roasted essence."

Marigold took a sip and let the beer roll over her tongue. Not just chocolate, she realized. *Dark* chocolate. With another flavor that brought to mind coffee. She could handle a porter. Finally, the surprise note that Kasima had mentioned hit her. "Cherries."

"Sour cherries." Kasima wiggled her eyebrows as if she were the cleverest girl in the world. Maybe she was—the porter was delicious and not at all heavy like Marigold had been expecting.

"This is good." Marigold took a mouthful this time, again savoring the flavors before swallowing. This time she caught the distinction. "Sour cherry. I totally get that."

Kasima beamed, and while they finished their drinks, Brian presented them each with a tumbler of ice water and a plate of pale, thin crackers.

"Was I supposed to bring the cheese?" Marigold joked, unsure of what was going on with the odd snack offering.

"Nope. Nothing salty at all between beers." Kasima shook her head. "The crackers are saltless to cleanse your palate."

The saltless crackers were dry and flavorless, but Marigold choked them down in the name of science, eager to try the next beer offering. The beer Brian poured this time was pale yellow in color and had a floral yet spicy aroma.

"This one's an American golden ale." Kasima watched as Marigold gave it a try.

"It's crisp," she said between sips. "And very easy to drink. This is something I would order with dinner. I bet it would pair well with hot wings too."

Kasima nodded as if in agreement with her assessment. "So, you like it?"

"I do." Marigold felt like this one could be the winner, but she intended to be fair and test the last beer as well. If nothing else, she was certainly getting an education that evening. She had been a beer drinker all her life—or at least since her late teens. How had she been so ignorant of the range of varieties out there?

The three indulged in the palate cleansing ritual again before Brian poured the final offering. This beer was more amber in color than the last, but still very translucent in the glass.

"I smell…pine," Marigold observed and felt quite sophisticated until her nose dipped a little too far into the glass and the liquid splashed up onto her skin.

Kasima giggled and swiped her thumb across the tip of Marigold's nose to banish the beer, but then she rested her palm against her cheek and their gazes met. And held.

Was it suddenly getting hot in the tasting kitchen?

Brian cleared his throat, breaking the spell. "I think I'll let the two of you take things from here. I promised I'd make it home in time for dinner tonight, and I don't want to make your mom mad." He winked, indicating that was a joke. "Marigold, thank you for the assist. I'm sure Kasima appreciates the help."

"Thank you for inviting me." Her cheeks were burning thinking about the moment he had caught them in, and once he left the room, she took a big gulp of her beer to cool off. "Oh, this is good. I taste…citrus?"

"You're getting good at this." Kasima grinned. She didn't seem as flustered as Marigold felt about the connection they'd just shared. Just cool and calm in her element—talking about beer. "This is a West Coast IPA. It's a style of beer originating in California, known for its bitterness, citrus and pine flavors, and a dry finish, often achieved through a process called 'dry hopping.' A true California beer."

"I really like this one too. It's very drinkable."

"It's beer." Kasima laughed and moved behind the bar to clear some of the empty glasses. "It's all drinkable."

"You know what I mean," Marigold tried again. "It goes down easy."

"Thank you. That's the goal. Did you want to try any of them again, or are you ready to vote?"

Marigold considered her next move. Based on the way she'd felt with Kasima's hand on her cheek just moments ago, she wasn't quite ready to call it a night. At the same time, drinking more alcohol on an empty stomach was probably a bad idea. The next time it could be more than just her nose that got sloshed with beer. "I'd definitely like another beer, but maybe with some food?"

"That's fair," Kasima agreed. "Any preliminary thoughts on which one you think we should brew for the Wildlife Rescue release? Or any questions?"

"All three were delicious," Marigold said diplomatically as they quickly cleaned up the little kitchen.

"And yet there can only be one winner," Kasima pointed out.

"What did you brew last year for the special release?"

"Last year we brewed a milkshake IPA." Kasima led the way from the brewery back toward the taproom.

Marigold was sure she'd misheard due to the crunching of gravel under their feet. Milkshake beer didn't make any sense—that couldn't be right. "What kind of IPA?"

"Milkshake. It's a hazy IPA brewed with milk sugar. Very trendy," Kasima answered matter-of-factly as she held the taproom door open. As Marigold passed through, Kasima put a hand on the small of her back to guide her to a table in the far corner of the room. It felt completely natural to have Kasima's hand on her as they crossed the room. Natural and quite pleasant. A gentle buzzing in her chest seemed to support the thought.

Her instinct was that milk and beer didn't mix, but she kept that to herself. She'd already learned she'd been leading a very sheltered beer life; she certainly couldn't speak to trends. "How'd it do as far as sales go?"

"It did fairly well." Kasima paused as the server approached and took their order, but once it was just the two of them again, she continued, "Honestly, it could've done better."

"My advice, as someone with a background in marketing, would be to avoid trendy this year. Go with something more universally familiar. To me, that rules out the porter."

"What?" Kasima looked incredulous. "Porters are classic beers."

Marigold shook her head. "People are afraid of it. Too dark."

"You just tasted it. Was it too bitter? No, it wasn't, and you liked it."

"That's true," Marigold confirmed. The last thing she wanted to do was offend. She was a guest, and she was only trying to be helpful. "But that's the way people will perceive it. With their preconceived notions. I think you should go with the West Coast IPA. Sell the public on it the same way you sold me, as 'a true California beer.' It seems fitting since this campaign is raising funds and awareness for SoCal Wildlife Rescue, doesn't it?"

Kasima seemed to consider that. "Background in marketing, eh?"

"Undergrad. I was a marketing major."

"And you really think the West Coast IPA is the way to go?"

"I do." Marigold nodded enthusiastically. The local angle could be a real boon for a marketing campaign. "Since the style has local roots, you can tie that into your marketing plan. Maybe put images of different local wildlife on the labels. Like a series—a 'collect them all' type of thing." The idea was gaining steam for her. "Is that something that's possible?"

"For sure." Kasima's brown eyes lit up with that flash of gold they got when she became passionate about something. Marigold had noticed it earlier during their tour of the brewery.

Clearly the idea was taking hold with Kasima, but they both sat silently while their sandwiches and beers were delivered to the table.

After they'd each taken a few bites, Kasima spoke again. "Now, when you say marketing plan…?"

"Well, what did you do last year?"

Kasima shrugged and wiped a napkin across the corner of her mouth to catch some wayward mustard. The mustard on her very sexy mouth. "We canned the beer with special labels, hung a banner out front to advertise, and sold it here out of the taproom."

"Oh, this year we can do a lot better than that."

"We?" Kasima's eyes looked hopeful.

Sure, work kept her busy, especially now with Ava Ashford on her roster. She knew that Kasima said she had no plans to build a romantic relationship between them, but helping out with the beer release was volunteering for a worthy cause. Plus, it would give her a little more time with Kasima, and maybe their relationship would move out of its fake era. Really, anything could happen. *Yeah, I'm doing this.* "Start brewing the West Coast IPA. I'll put some ideas together, and we'll talk again in a few days."

CHAPTER TWELVE

Once the mash for the new batch of West Coast IPA was resting in the tank Monday morning, Kasima sat in her office working on the sketch she'd started the night before. Over the weekend she and Marigold had texted sporadically, sharing ideas for the special release. They still hadn't come up with a good name, although they had agreed it should either be regional or animal-related and still keep with the Enchanted Hops Hollywood-themed branding. Since Marigold would be out of town for the next couple of days, occupied with her actual job of talent management, Kasima decided to get to work on designing the labels.

The one she was currently giving her attention to was a great horned owl. It was an abstract version of the large bird in bright blues against a yellow-and red-hued background. Attention-grabbing, but still animal-centric. She would run this one past Marigold first, then once she had her opinion she would create three more featuring animals native to southern California that the wildlife rescue served.

After Marigold had agreed to help with marketing for the special brew, they had moved on to other topics of discussion while they had finished dinner. Marigold was smart and interesting and knew how to keep a conversation going. That was especially refreshing to Kasima, although as she reflected on the feeling, she wondered if maybe good one-on-one conversation was just something her life had been lacking lately. Not that she didn't spend plenty of time with her family. She always had Spence to bounce ideas off of at the brewery if she needed to. But there was something satisfying about a cozy conversation in a quiet, dimly lit corner with a lovely woman. It was a feeling she had nearly forgotten, but it was reawakened in those sixty minutes she had spent with Marigold over pub sandwiches and craft beer. Additionally, she could not stop thinking about the way the muscles in Marigold's back had felt relaxing against her hand as they had walked through the taproom. She hadn't felt that instantly comfortable with a woman since…no. She wasn't going to let her thoughts go there. But still, it was like Marigold had sunk into her touch. Yielding to her. Very…sexy.

When Kasima realized she was sinking her teeth into the colored pencil she was meant to be sketching an owl with, she shook her head to bring herself back to reality. She needed to stop herself from going too far down that pathway of thought. There was nothing romantic or sexual truly happening between the two of them. Their relationship had been entirely an illusion to fulfill a need. A fantasy, nothing more. Although she appreciated Marigold's help with the marketing campaign, she did worry that she may have been steamrolled by the situation into assisting with it. Marigold was a professional in public relations and her guidance on the project was invaluable to the brewery, but Kasima hoped she didn't feel obligated to volunteer based on their fake date arrangement. As far as she was concerned, that had come to an end once they had left the Wildlife Rescue fundraiser.

Of course, there was still the matter of letting her parents know that she wasn't really in a relationship with Marigold. That they weren't girlfriends. A fake breakup, so to speak. She would need to talk to them soon and clear things up. Maybe that would clear her conscience.

The squeak of her office door opening drew her out of her thoughts.

"Knock knock." Her dad poked his head into the office before entering with his entire body, like he wanted to announce himself before being completely present in the room. "Oh hey, what are you working on?"

"Label design. This will be one of four, I hope," she explained as he approached her desk to get a better look. "Like a series. Marigold's idea."

A knowing smile graced her dad's face. "So, she agreed to help you on this. I'm glad. You two really seem to work well together."

She sensed he meant more than just they worked well at marketing together. He was commenting on the two of them as a couple. An ember of guilt burned in her belly. It was time to come clean about the situation. "Dad, about that—"

"Honey, you don't have to be embarrassed about the way you two were looking at each other all gaga-eyed in the test kitchen the other night. It's perfectly normal."

Oh no. He was taking this in the total opposite direction. He sounded like he was about to give her some kind of "the birds and the bees" speech. *And what the hell was he talking about anyway? Gaga-eyed?*

"No, Dad. It's not that. I need to explain. Me and Marigold, we're…" How was she going to do this? How was she going to tell his happy face that she and Marigold weren't actually a couple? That they'd actually been lying to him and the rest of the family this whole time. And that it had all been her idea to do so.

He put his big, gentle hand on her shoulder and gave it a tender squeeze, the same way he used to show he was proud of her when she was a kid. "You don't have to explain anything. Your mom and I are so happy for you. You know that we've been really worried about you. We understand how very much you loved Libby, and—"

"Dad." Now it was her turn to cut him off midsentence. She could handle a lot of things, but she just couldn't talk about Libby with him. Not right then when only a few moments prior she had been hyperfocused on how it had felt to touch Marigold's back.

The sick feeling swirling in her stomach wormed its way into her throat, making her blink back the threat of tears. She had to shut the conversation down. "It's fine. Marigold and I are fine. And we'll keep you in the loop on the marketing stuff. But right now, I need to get back into the brewery. It's just about time for the mash to go into the boiler, and I want to keep a close eye on what gets added when during the boil."

Steering the conversation back to business helped. It grounded her. She'd messed up on her intended Marigold messaging, but she would still give her dad something he could be proud of—a successful brew for the wildlife rescue organization. "I think we can totally blow last year's sales out of the water with the West Coast IPA. The proceeds should provide a sizable donation."

A look of confusion clouded his expression for a brief moment, but then his easy smile reappeared. "Okay, kid. Don't let me stand in the way of progress."

As she hurried out of her office to the brewery floor, her momentary relief began to fade. She had avoided a painful topic, but she had failed to be honest with her dad about her relationship—or lack thereof—with Marigold. She was still going to have to make things right. She sighed. *Next time.*

CHAPTER THIRTEEN

Marigold looked on from the wings of the sound stage while Ava chatted away with Calvin Long, the dark-haired, lopsided-smile host of The After Hours Show. It was the last stop on a two-day tour of daytime talk and late-night shows that had started in New York City and, after a quick stop in Chicago, brought them back to Los Angeles.

Ava had done surprisingly well at sticking to the scripted answers she had been given at the start of the circuit, so as she launched into the well-rehearsed response recounting a semihumorous story about her audition for the role of Dakota Oakley, Marigold felt safe to let her mind wander to Kasima and the special brew marketing efforts.

During her downtime on the trip she had come up with a few ideas for an effective, yet economical promotion, and she hoped to schedule some time later in the week to meet with Kasima and talk them through.

The first order of business needed in order to kick off the marketing plan would be to come up with the name for the beer.

She had taken care not to overstep—it was important to Kasima that the name was something that fit Enchanted Hops's overall branding, so Marigold wanted to give her the space and time to get it right. Kasima had already come up with a great design idea for the labels. Marigold smiled as she recalled the excited, emoji-filled text message she'd received from Kasima along with the picture of the owl sketch. They would need to put their heads together and really get to work after Ava's apology tour concluded, but overall, things were coming along quite well.

She was glad she'd volunteered her time to the SoCal Wildlife Rescue special release. The change of focus from talent to product was oddly gratifying. And if it gave her the chance to spend a little more time with Kasima, all the better. Maybe along the way she would find a way to knock down those high walls Kasima had built up around herself.

She had spent more time than she cared to admit over the past several days thinking about the excitement that had shot straight through her when Kasima had touched her cheek that day during their beer tasting. Such a simple gesture with such tremendous impact. Marigold wanted—no, needed—more of that feeling. Even just thinking now about staring into those gorgeous nut-brown eyes, so rich and satisfying—like that porter Kasima had introduced her to—made her nipples go hard under her shirt.

She was fanning her suddenly warm face with her hand when she noticed Ava had hopped up from her chair on stage and was gesturing to the audience.

"Come on, say it with me!" she bellowed to the full theater. "Lez ride!"

Wait. This was not in the agreed-upon script.

Marigold grabbed the stage manager's arm and yanked him close. "I want my client off the stage *now*. Go to break."

The manager shrugged out of her grasp and shook his head. "That's not your call to make, lady."

Her stomach sank as she watched Ava jump up and down, waving the red ruffled blouse she'd been wearing mere seconds earlier in the air above her head, her young body gyrating and threatening to pop right out of the jet black bustier that was now serving as a top. "Louder!" she jeered. "Lez ride!"

Marigold's instinct was to run out there, preferably with a blanket to cover the kid up, and carry her off the stage. Where was one of those hooks they used to use to yank people back into the wings in the days of vaudeville? Hell, at this point, she'd settle for a Gong Show gong.

Fortunately, Calvin Long seemed to recognize that he was losing control of his show and announced they were going to break.

Marigold shook her blazer off as she rushed the stage and threw it over Ava's shoulders. What she really wanted to do was wring the kid's neck. This was supposed to be a tour of atonement, not the inciting of some kind of queer lady riot. But as weird as it felt to roll with the punches, she remembered Allison's command to handle Ava with kid gloves and tried her best to do so. The situation was under control; no further reprimand was necessary. It was time to call it a night and get her client home.

"Ride's over," she quipped as she pulled Ava backstage.

CHAPTER FOURTEEN

"Do you think your dad would be open to holding a launch party here in the taproom?" Marigold dragged a french fry through the puddle of ketchup on her plate. She had met Kasima in the taproom Wednesday afternoon to talk marketing strategy and have a quick bite.

Kasima stared at her mouth as she finally popped the tasty treat in it. What was it about this woman's plump lips that was just so fascinating? "I think he'd totally go for it. You know how Dad loves a good party."

"Great. I'll put together a presser about it. We'll make the product reveal a big deal—we'll livestream it too. Broaden our reach and maybe give consumers who don't make it to the launch party a little FOMO. We can launch the product that night at the party and then with a little luck, continue to bring people into Enchanted Hops to pick up the special brew over the next couple of months until the supply runs out. Maybe when they come in they'll eat and drink here as well. A win-win."

"A product reveal like the tech companies do when they launch the latest and greatest phone? That sounds…glamorous." Maybe too glamorous. Kasima had visions of a swanky event juxtaposed with their casual-style taproom. The two images didn't exactly mesh. Enchanted Hops was just a local brewery, not a world-wide obsession. "Do you think we can pull that off?"

Marigold seemed to sense where her mind was. "We'll keep it casual, I promise. Everything we do will stay in line with Enchanted Hops Brewing Company's branding."

"That sounds great." She pulled up her calendar on her tablet. "We should have the first full batch canned and ready to sell in three weeks. Any time after that will work."

They had agreed on the name Hooray For Howlywood for the West Coast IPA only two days earlier after several text exchanges of various animal and Hollywood combinations, including Hootywood & Lion and Born To Be Wild.

"Let's plan the party for a Thursday." Marigold leaned across the table to get a better view of the schedule. "That way you'll have some buzz generated and you may get a bump in sales from the reveal all weekend."

"Damn, you're good."

Marigold sat back in her seat and a sexy smile played across her lips. "This is what I do. I mean, basically, though my job is actually more about promoting people than products."

"I know what you said before, but I still think working with celebrities sounds exciting."

"It truly is exciting sometimes." Marigold shrugged, but her satisfied grin didn't fade. "Other times it's a little more like celebrity wrangling. Feels like I've been doing a lot of that lately with Ava Ashford."

"Ava Ashford?" Kasima twirled a fry between her fingers and tried to recall where she'd heard that name before. "I've definitely heard of her, but I don't know what she does."

"She's the star of that television show *Homestead Hollow*. Ever see it?" At the shake of Kasima's head, Marigold continued, "The premise is that in 1909 the Earth's moon split into two, causing a near apocalypse, and almost all of humanity was wiped out.

The show takes place a year after, in the Wild West of what was formerly the United States. Ava's character, Dakota Oakley—the granddaughter of Annie Oakley—leads a band of survivors as they try to survive and rebuild civilization."

Kasima considered the information for a beat. "It's an apocalyptic Wild West show in which the Earth has two moons?"

"Yeah." Marigold seemed to understand her confusion. "I know, it's an interesting concept. But viewers love it. I think it's because they're so invested in the characters. Oh, and there are werewolves."

Kasima choked on her beer. The premise of this show was getting weirder with every word Marigold said. "Are you mentioning the werewolves to help me understand the popularity of the show?"

"No." Marigold laughed and her deep-green eyes sparkled. "I just forgot to mention it in my original summary, and I thought it was an important plot point."

"I'm sorry, but the werewolves make it sound even more ridiculous."

"I feel obligated to point out that I don't write the show."

"So, you think it's a little ridiculous too. You admit you think the product you're promoting is ridiculous." Kasima couldn't resist the urge to tease her—she wanted to hear more of her joyful laugh. She gasped dramatically. "How do I know you don't think our product is ridiculous?"

It had the desired effect—Marigold's eyes twinkled along with her laugh again. "First, I don't actually promote the show, I only promote Ava. Second, I love your beer." She took a drink of Hollywood Haze as if to emphasize her point. Her expression softened when she continued, "Plus, I'm a big fan of the people who make it."

With that one simple statement a jolt of excitement shot through Kasima. Marigold was a big fan. Of her. It was quite flattering. And surprisingly pleasing. "Well, the person—people—who make it are big fans of you as well." God, she was terrible at flirting. She so rarely did it these days.

Marigold didn't seem to mind, though. She bit her bottom lip, tilted her head to the side, and regarded her. Kasima's core hummed happily in response. "Seriously, *Homestead Hollow* is an entertaining show. You should watch it sometime. Maybe we could even watch it together."

Kasima was really starting to enjoy the time she was spending with Marigold working on the marketing campaign, and she wouldn't mind hanging out with her on a more extracurricular basis. "That sounds good. We can watch the Wild West werewolf show together sometime." She still felt she needed to add, "Strictly as friends, of course."

The qualification didn't seem to deter Marigold. "Just so you know, the werewolves aren't really what the show is about. It's really about Dakota Oakley and her mission to save the world."

Kasima nodded. "You did a great job of turning that around to promote your client." She couldn't stop her teasing grin. "I'm impressed."

"Listen, Ava Ashford is definitely a handful as a client, but she's a client nonetheless. It's my job to do my best by her." Marigold appeared thoughtful as she chewed on the last fry from the plate. Their meeting was almost over. "Can I be honest?"

"Of course."

"Yes, promoting my client is my job, but I truly want to see Ava succeed." Marigold's green eyes were sincere. She really was beautiful. "There's something about the kid that makes me want to cheer for her and protect her a little too. I can't quite put my finger on it, but it's there."

"It's probably that exact gut feeling that makes you so good at your job."

The blush that rose in Marigold's cheeks when their gazes met again sent another crackle of excitement through Kasima, and even though her brain warned her to cool down because there could be nothing more than friendship between them, she still enjoyed it.

But maybe she shouldn't have agreed to any extracurricular activities. They should probably just stick to working on marketing the beer. Nothing more. She didn't want to give Marigold the wrong idea and lead her on in any way. She would definitely be much more careful going forward.

* * *

When Kasima offered to walk her to her car after their planning session, Marigold gladly accepted. She wasn't ready for their time together to come to an end, but she understood that Kasima had other job duties besides planning for this one event. It had only been a week and a half since she'd agreed to assist with promotion for the SoCal Wildlife Rescue release, and she didn't regret signing on one bit. Doing something to promote a good cause was a pleasant respite from promoting strong-willed, egotistical clients. In addition to that, she was just plain having fun hanging out with Kasima.

She still had a couple of marketing tricks up her sleeve for the Hooray For Howlywood release, but she wanted to have all her ducks in a row before presenting the ideas to Kasima. The last thing she wanted to do was to set her up for disappointment. But without any new marketing plans to discuss, there was no beer-related reason for them to meet again any time soon. Yes, Kasima said they could watch *Homestead Hollow* together sometime, but she hadn't actually committed to that time, and that left Marigold feeling vaguely glum. Luckily as she was loading her tote bags into the back of her Mini Cooper, she spotted an old takeout receipt from one of her favorite restaurants on the floor mat, and inspiration struck.

"Have you ever eaten at Xenia's Taverna?"

Kasima's brows scrunched together as if she was trying to place the name. "I don't think so. Is it around here?"

"Santa Monica. Do you like Greek food?"

"I think so." Kasima shrugged apologetically. "I like the spanakopita from the frozen section at Costco. I'm not sure I've ever tried authentic Greek food."

"Xenia's Taverna makes the best spanakopita," Marigold gushed. Even though they'd just enjoyed a bite while party planning, her mouth began to water as she thought about some of her favorite Greek dishes. "You'll love the food there. I promise it's a million times better than any frozen Costco offering. What are you doing Friday?"

"Friday? I don't know. Did you want to get together to talk more about the release event?"

She could sense the "I don't date" speech incoming, so Marigold launched a preemptive strike. "We're friends, Kasima. We can make plans for dinner just because. Or we can get together to watch *Homestead Hollow* just for the hell of it. Those are the kinds of things friends do. We don't have to be talking about Hooray For Howlywood every time we hang out."

To her relief, Kasima's expression relaxed noticeably. "You know, you're right. Let's have dinner at Xenia's Taverna. Introduce me to good Greek food."

Marigold promised to make reservations for seven o'clock Friday and they said their goodbyes. As she drove off the Enchanted Hops campus, it felt as if her lungs were filled with helium, giving her a happy floating feeling. Whether it was from having plans to visit one of her favorite restaurants or the prospect of hanging out with Kasima again, she didn't know. Or necessarily care.

CHAPTER FIFTEEN

Friday evening, just as Marigold was about to step through the front doors of Xenia's Taverna where she was supposed to meet Kasima, her phone rang. Kasima.

She chose to pick up the call outside, hoping she'd have better reception there or, at the very least, be able to hear more clearly without the din of the dinner crowd.

"I'm really sorry," Kasima said as soon as Marigold said hello. "There's an emergency at the brewery and I can't leave."

"An emergency at the brewery," Marigold repeated. She knew Kasima was still going to be weird about hanging out together outside of working on the campaign, but she didn't have to lie about it. She took a deep breath before continuing. She was disappointed, but really, Kasima didn't owe her anything. If she didn't want to hang out, then that was that. "I guess our seven o'clock dinner is off then."

"I'm afraid so," Kasima confirmed. "One of the old fermentation tanks went kaput and if we don't get it serviced immediately, we risk losing all of the product in it."

Work emergencies happened—no one knew that better than Marigold—but it had been hard enough to convince Kasima to make these plans in the first place. A kaput fermentation tank felt just a little too convenient. "Is *kaput* a technical beer-brewing term?" she joked half-heartedly.

"It's a more gentle term than some of the words I want to say about the situation," Kasima groused. Marigold had never heard her sound anything less than sunny. It was striking. "I'm stuck sitting in the old tank room waiting for the service guy to show up, and who knows how long that will take since it's after hours."

Marigold glanced at her watch. It was nearly seven o'clock. Her stomach was already rumbling with hunger. If Kasima had to wait for this dude to show up, they might not get to eat for hours. They might as well just cancel. "I guess I should go in and let them know we won't be making our reservation."

"Just because I can't make it doesn't mean you shouldn't enjoy dinner at Xenia's. Seriously. Enjoy. You can even send me a pic of your food to make me wither away with envy that you're enjoying a delicious meal while I'm stuck sitting in the stupid tank room, bored out of my mind just sitting and waiting."

At precisely that moment a patron exited the restaurant and the tantalizing aroma of garlic, oregano, and thyme wafted out to the sidewalk. Marigold was already there and had a reservation, she may as well eat.

"The company won't be nearly as engaging, but a gal does have to eat." She'd probably return a few emails on her tablet as she dined since it would be a table for one now, but better than going home to forage through her cabinets for something worthy of ingesting.

Before they said their goodbyes, Kasima apologized again, her voice small and not at all representative of the woman Marigold knew her to be. Was it because she was ashamed to be pulling a last-minute cancellation on a friend? Or because she'd never intended to show up for dinner in the first place?

Marigold shoved her phone into her tote and blew out a long sigh. What was she getting so bent out of shape for? Sometimes things happen and plans have to be canceled. Reading more into it wasn't exactly being a good friend to Kasima.

As she stepped through the front door of Xenia's Taverna and breathed in that heavenly aroma her stomach gave another hungry grumble. Kasima was going to miss out on quite a treat, and she was probably pretty damn hungry by now too.

No, Marigold thought. A good friend wouldn't leave the other one sitting alone, bored out of her mind because she was having a crisis at work.

She approached the host desk to let them know the change in plans.

* * *

A little over an hour had passed since Kasima had hung up with Marigold, and, as she'd predicted, she was already bored out of her skull. She could only scroll through so much social media and play so many games of Candy Crush before she wanted to bang her head against the cement block wall of the old tank room.

It was her own fault really. She should have scheduled a service visit weeks ago when she suspected a problem. Instead, she'd put it off while she got caught up in the special release promotion with Marigold.

She stood and did a few jumping jacks to loosen her legs, which were cramped and achy after sitting on the metal folding chair she'd dragged out of the maintenance closet at the far end of the L-shaped room. It seemed like it would be better than sitting on the cement floor, but her stiff joints were telling her it wasn't better by much.

On top of the boredom and the aches in her legs, she couldn't quite shake the feeling that Marigold was upset with her for canceling their dinner plans and that made her empty stomach twist with worry. One would think that working with clients like Ava Ashford, Marigold would understand that sometimes work emergencies arose and plans had to be changed. But when they spoke on the phone earlier, she had seemed…annoyed? Disappointed? Kasima wasn't sure. Either way, the reaction had been disheartening. Marigold hadn't tried to reschedule their dinner for another day or time. She'd simply ended the call as if she had given up on her and their friendship.

Kasima hadn't wanted to cancel on her, especially not at the last minute like that. She'd actually been looking forward to their meal at Xenia's Taverna all day. Not just because she was looking forward to the food there either. It had been a long time since she felt as comfortable with someone as she did with Marigold. There was something about her willingness to go along with whatever came her way and the ability to pivot when needed to make something work that set Kasima's mind at ease and made her feel safe. That vibe had been glaringly absent during their phone call earlier, though.

Was Marigold upset with her about this? Her scalp prickled. She didn't want Marigold to think she was some kind of a jerk who didn't care about other people's feelings. What if Marigold had decided she didn't want to hang out together outside of working on the Wildlife Rescue release anymore—that she wanted to stick to business activities only? Kasima was already starting to dread what would happen once the release party was over and they didn't have to spend time together. She would definitely feel a void without Marigold in her life. Without Marigold's *friendship* in her life, she corrected herself.

She shook her head to clear it and reached for her phone. This was ridiculous. She should just call Marigold, apologize again for canceling at the last minute, and clear this all up. Get things between them back on track.

But Marigold didn't pick up the call. There was only endless ringing, followed by a very businesslike voice mail greeting. Kasima clicked off the call without leaving a message and began pacing the length of the tank room. This couldn't be a good sign—Marigold always had her phone close by. Was she dodging her calls now?

Before she could fire off a follow-up text, she heard the exterior door of the tank room open. The service guy. At least the waiting-around portion of the evening was over. Once he got started on the tank repairs, she could retreat to her office and figure out what to do about the Marigold situation.

"Hello? A little help, please?" The voice that called out from around the bend where the door was located out of Kasima's line of sight was definitely not that of the service dude.

"Marigold?" Kasima rushed to her and quickly grabbed one of the takeout bags she was balancing on her hip while she attempted to enter the space without the heavy tank room door closing on her. "What are you doing here?"

"You couldn't make it to Xenia's Taverna, so I brought Xenia's Taverna to you."

Kasima inhaled the warm, spicy aroma coming from the contents of the bag she was holding and her stomach growled in anticipation.

"You brought me food?"

"I brought both of us food." Marigold set her bags down and reached into her giant tote. "And a blanket to spread out for us to picnic on. I didn't know what dish you'd want, so I got a few things for us to share."

Kasima watched in delight as she spread out the blanket and arranged the takeout containers. Her chest swelled with gratitude. "You didn't have to do all this."

"I knew you were bored, and I figured you were hungry." Marigold shrugged and gave her a tired smile. "What are friends for, right?"

After what was no doubt a full day of work with a high-maintenance client and after having dinner plans changed on her at the very last minute, Marigold had still been kind enough to think about Kasima and take care of her. The considerate act warmed her heart and buoyed her own tired spirit. Overcome with appreciation and possibly by the delicious aroma of the food, Kasima impulsively pulled Marigold into a hug. Her throat was thick with emotion as she murmured into Marigold's shoulder, "Thank you."

* * *

Twenty minutes later with a belly full of spanakopita, keftedes, and pita and hummus, Kasima sighed contentedly and leaned back on her elbows. Despite the hard floor underneath their blanket, if she closed her eyes she could picture the two of them on an actual picnic—outside—somewhere green like Griffith

Park instead of confined by the cement block walls of the old tank room. A picnic in Griffith Park would be a fun way to spend a day together. Maybe they could do a little hiking there too. Or biking, if Marigold preferred.

"I hope you saved room for dessert," Marigold said, bringing her back to the moment. "I ordered us some baklava."

"There's dessert?" Kasima sat up again and reached for a square of the flaky treat from the box Marigold was offering.

Marigold seemed to enjoy the baklava as much as she did, polishing off her square, then licking a wayward smear of honey from her deep-mauve-manicured fingertip. She moaned with obvious pleasure as she savored the bite.

A flutter of excitement stirred in Kasima's core that had nothing to do with the decadent walnut and cinnamon flavors in the treat. It was all she could do to tear her gaze away from Marigold's plump, scarlet lips. Even when she managed to look away, need continued to tug somewhere behind her belly button. She hadn't felt this compelled to jump a woman's bones in a damn long time. She took one more glance at that sexy mouth and, as if mesmerized, leaned close enough to smell Marigold's green-tea shampoo. An absolutely delectable perfume. Suddenly she wanted nothing more than to kiss Marigold. To take her in her arms and press her lips to her. Taste the sweet baklava on her lips. But she couldn't do that.

A kiss would likely lead to two. And then to *more*. The only times she'd had *more* in the past five years were strictly one-and-dones. Or, in a couple of cases, a few-and-dones. No commitments, no romantic ties at all. Simply enjoyable nights—moments of pleasure to satisfy a need—between two people who knew damn well that when the sun came up they would part ways amicably and move on with their lives. No strings. No promises. Nothing at all that would put her heart at risk of being broken.

But with Marigold there were already strings. They were entangled in the charade that they were a couple, and they were working together on this project. They were eating a meal that Marigold had gone out of her way to bring to her. They…were friends.

She knew she shouldn't let herself be tempted, yet here she was, unabashedly tempted, her whole body pulsing with excitement. What if she allowed herself one quick kiss to get the curiosity out of her system? Her gaze locked on Marigold's plump lips. Just one little…

"Hello? Kasima?" a deep male voice called from across the room. It was Joe, the tank service provider she'd been waiting for, arriving just in time to break the spell she'd fallen under and keep her from making a choice she would most certainly regret.

She jumped to her feet, brushed some crumbs from her T-shirt, and strode across the room to take care of business. *Actual* business.

What had she been thinking anyway? Sure, Marigold had the most irresistible lips Kasima had ever seen, and she'd come all the way to the brewery to provide company and food in her time of need. And, yes, Kasima's heart was still pounding at the prospect of making out with her right there on the tank room floor. But none of that meant Kasima should act on it. She didn't need to make herself vulnerable like that again. She knew better. *Hell, you're supposed to be working anyway!* She fixed her face into an all-business smile and greeted Joe.

* * *

While Kasima spoke with the tank repair person, Marigold pulled out her tablet and scrolled through social media. She needed something to distract her from the humming in her chest that had kicked up while the two of them were enjoying dessert. She knew damn well that it wasn't the baklava—as delicious as it was—that had her body all abuzz. *This is not the way a friend would act*, she mentally scolded herself. Although maybe if they hung out enough Kasima's feelings would change, and they could have an actual real romantic relationship.

Before she had too long to linger on that thought, Kasima returned and sat back down on the blanket with her.

"Did you seriously just jump right back into work?" Kasima popped another bite of baklava into her mouth and frowned while she chewed. "I was gone for like five minutes."

"I'm just checking Ava's socials."

"You're creeping on Ava Ashford," Kasima accused, but the sparkle in her eyes made it clear she was teasing.

Marigold was quick to defend herself. "I'm not creeping. I'm *assessing*. There's a big difference."

"Oh yeah, sure." Kasima's exaggerated nod wasn't convincing. "Do you do this for all of your clients?"

"I don't, but someone at the agency does. Actually, most of our clients don't handle their own social media at all. That job is normally assigned to one of the junior associates in the office. But according to my boss, Ava is too precious to be treated like everyone else. Ava worked it into her contract that she will keep full control of all of her socials." Marigold sighed. Another allowance that would normally never fly with the agency if it was anyone other than Ava Ashford. So ridiculous and such damn risky business.

"Even though we have junior associates keeping a constant eye on it to alert me if anything goes sideways, I like to check it out myself occasionally. If for no other reason than to keep up-to-date on where the kid's head is at. I mean, look at this." She handed the tablet to Kasima and waited for her to read the entire rambling post.

"What exactly is hashtag Real Entourage?"

"It's her half-baked plan to have a reality TV show about her half-baked friend group. I suspect she thinks she can drum up fan support for the idea and make it happen. Like, social media manifesting or some such shit."

Kasima handed the tablet back. "Is it an idea worth exploring, this reality TV thing? They look like an interesting cast of characters. Young, hip, a fun friend group."

"They may be young and hip, but they're awful friends," Marigold said as she clicked the device off and returned it to her tote bag. "It seems that, more often than not, any time Ava's acting out and making crap choices, this group is in tow. On top of the questionable behavior they always seem to be present for, I get the feeling they're just using her. She seems to be the one picking up the check for all of the group's adventures."

"Well, that sucks. Poor kid."

"She could just tell them to get lost, but she won't. She likes the attention and adoration, no matter how manufactured it might be. They're playing her like a fiddle." Marigold shook her head. "I swear, half of my job is protecting my clients from themselves. That's enough shop talk. For me anyway. What's the story with the fermentation tank?"

"Joe can do a patch on it, but it's going to need to be replaced." Kasima waved a dismissive hand in the air at Marigold's sympathetic frown. "I knew that news was coming. It's okay. But the patch will take him a little over an hour, so I'm going to be here a while yet. You don't have to stick around—you've done so much for me tonight already. Thank you, by the way."

"Are you kidding me? I had a blast. I can't remember the last time I had a picnic. And I never had one amid the fermentation tanks of a brewery before."

"It is a one-of-a-kind experience." Kasima grinned.

"Exactly. And we still have some baklava left, so I'm not leaving yet. Why don't you tell me how the production of Hooray For Howlywood is coming along while we have another piece?"

Marigold happily munched on a second helping of dessert while Kasima updated her, those brown eyes of hers growing brighter and more passion-filled with every word. As tired as she was, she could listen to Kasima talk about beer all night once she got going. Cement floor or not—sitting shoulder to shoulder with Kasima, she was in her happy place.

Her happy, totally just friends place.

CHAPTER SIXTEEN

Kasima settled in on Marigold's indigo sofa with a big bowl of freshly popped, buttery popcorn between them. Most of the living room was styled in rich creams and tan hues. This piece of furniture was the only outlier, providing a contrast to its surroundings. It somehow felt very Marigold to her. Just when you thought you knew her—boom—there was something to surprise and delight you that you weren't expecting. And Kasima was learning that she really enjoyed discovering each new facet of Marigold. Things like the fact that she watched *Homestead Hollow* not just because her client was in it, but because she actually liked the weird-ass Wild West apocalypse show.

"Now tell me again," Kasima said, pulling a chunky taupe knit throw from the arm of the sofa over her legs. It was not so much for warmth as it was a feeling of security. The subject matter of *Homestead Hollow* low-key freaked her out. "Dakota Oakley is leading a group of apocalypse survivors in a fight against werewolves?"

"No, no." Marigold shook her head and grabbed a handful of popcorn. "You're missing a lot of nuance in that summary. The werewolves don't even make an appearance until a few episodes into the season. You have to start from square one. The Earth's moon has split into two moons and that's what caused the apocalypse. You'll see."

"I'm gonna stop you right there." Kasima cracked open her beer. "Why would the moon split into two? How could that be? Like, what caused it? It just doesn't make sense."

"I'm going to stop *you* right there," Marigold countered. "I'm going to ask you to suspend disbelief, open your mind, and just accept this fact: the moon has split into two, setting in motion an apocalypse. Everything else will fall into line after that. Just watch." She pressed play on the remote and leaned back into the couch cushions, making it clear they were done with the prescreening Q and A session.

Kasima took a long swallow of beer and watched the opening scene unfold. The two moons were in the evening sky, and the hero, Dakota Oakley, was having a conversation with a fellow survivor of the apocalypse that provided context but—she couldn't help noticing—no actual explanation or science-based reason for the state of affairs. Then the opening title sequence began.

"The theme song kind of gives the vibe of a spooky, Western version of 'Come On Get Happy,' though, right?"

"Would you hush?" Marigold laughed and bumped their shoulders together. "I'm glad you're opening your mind, but nothing about this is giving off Partridge Family vibes. Just watch."

The attempts at humor were purely a defense mechanism, but certainly within her control if only she knew what she was dealing with. *Homestead Hollow* seemed like the kind of show that would be one surprise after the next.

"Just tell me if I should be expecting any jump scares."

Marigold turned to her with a precious expression and put a reassuring hand on her thigh. The warmth of her touch bolstered Kasima's brave face efforts. "No jump scares. Wait. No. Not in the first episode. I don't think."

"Come on," Kasima whined. That answer wasn't exactly reassuring. Outside the sun was setting, and without natural light the room was growing darker by the minute, enhancing the spooky mood. "Are you kidding me right now?"

"A little bit." Her cocky grin made her eyes shine. "But don't worry, I'm right here to keep you safe."

"I'm going to hold you to that." Kasima put the bowl of popcorn on her lap, scooted closer to Marigold until their hips were touching, and braced herself for whatever chills and thrills *Homestead Hollow* was about to deliver.

* * *

Three episodes and two beers after snuggling up on the couch to watch *Homestead Hollow*, Marigold paused the stream. "Well? What do you think?"

Kasima shook her head. "I can't believe I'm going to say this, but…I'm hooked."

"It's the characters, right?" She could totally understand Kasima's disbelief. The premise was more than a little questionable, but still, the show was addicting. That was evident in the way the viewership had grown by leaps and bounds over the course of that first season. "Dakota's best friend, Brisa, is such a fearless badass, and Frank and Miles are perfect comic relief. I kind of love them."

"I know," Kasima enthusiastically agreed. "And the will-they-won't-they between Dakota and Charlotte is done really well. God, I hope they get together."

Not wanting to spoil the story, Marigold tried to keep her expression neutral. "Guess you're going to have to keep watching to find out."

"I'll tell you what really surprised me. Ava Ashford might be a handful as a client, but she's really good as Dakota Oakley. The girl can act."

"Agreed. She's always been good, a real natural. And it's only been recently—definitely since she's taken on this role—that she's been giving me a hard time. When she was younger, she was quiet, reserved even. She's nineteen now, and I don't know if this is some kind of late-stage teenage rebellion or what, but I'm just hoping she gets over it soon."

"Hard to imagine the hard-as-nails woman I just saw on the screen as Dakota Oakley ever being quiet or reserved," Kasima observed. "She truly seems like a rough, tough, Wild West cowgirl."

"That speaks to the good acting, I suppose." Marigold laughed. "Her grandmother raised her right here in sunny La La Land, California."

"Okay, public relations professional." Kasima laughed along with her. "That sounds like an official Ava Ashford statement."

"Well, it's the truth, just with a few bits left out." Marigold chewed the inside of her cheek and considered how much to divulge. It was all public knowledge—there if anyone should choose to dig for it. But shining a light on a client's personal life was completely contradictory to Marigold's job duties. Still, this wasn't speaking to the general public. It was only Kasima, the woman who had spent the last three hours pressed up against her on the couch. She was her friend. Potentially even more than that. Who knew? There was definitely a vibe between them, no matter how many times Kasima insisted they could be nothing more. Anyway, for now that was what they were…friends.

"Ava's grandmother got custody of her when she was young, three or four. Her parents had drug-use issues which led to her mother dying from an overdose and her father landing in prison. He was killed in a fight only a few weeks after he was locked up. It's such a sad story. But Anita, Ava's grandmother, has always been there for her."

Kasima nodded. "Sounds like Ava is lucky to have her in her life."

"She really is." Marigold thought sadly of how the only living family member she had left in her own life was her mother and how many years had been wasted—lost—in their relationship. "Anita got her into acting classes and vocal lessons mainly as a way to keep Ava busy, but it turned out the girl had talent. I think Anita really wanted her to be too busy to find the kind of problems her parents had faced, which was understandable. Ava did a lot of commercials and bit parts over the years. *Homestead Hollow* is her first big role. The agency has managed her career all this time and she never gave us trouble like she has lately." Saying it out loud made the connection between the role and the behavior seem even more obvious.

"So, maybe it's the new fame behind the behavior." Kasima seemed to be drawing the same conclusion. "I can imagine that kind of thing—the sudden popularity and having fans—could take some getting used to."

"I hope she gets used to it soon." Marigold pulled a throw pillow onto her lap, then hugged it to her chest, resting her chin on it. Her eyes were starting to get that gritty feeling that set in when she was tired. It wasn't that late, but she'd had a couple of long days of work and was already feeling sleepy. "Because between middle of the night rescue missions and the resulting public relations spinning, Ava Ashford is running me ragged."

Kasima snaked a comforting arm around her and pulled her in for a side hug. The gesture made Marigold long to fall asleep in her arms. Cozy. Comfortable. Safe. It was hard to believe, not to mention disheartening, that Kasima didn't feel the same way, but she'd been clear about her boundaries. Marigold knew she had to respect them if she wanted to continue to have any sort of relationship with her. For now, she would take what she could get and just enjoy the moment.

CHAPTER SEVENTEEN

"These are awesome." Marigold seemed to take her time studying each sketch, touching each one in turn, tracing her fingers along the bold colorful lines that made up the images. Kasima had invited her to stop by the brewery to check out all four of her completed label designs. "Oh my God, a mountain lion? Did you choose this one because of me?"

"I did. The proud mountain lion." Kasima couldn't explain why the joy on Marigold's face when she discovered the big cat had been selected especially for her set off butterflies in her belly. Nor could she explain why they seemed to multiply tenfold when Marigold pulled her into an excited hug. "You'll notice I've got my little opossum represented as well."

Marigold released her and turned her gaze back to the sketches. "These are going to be popular. I think we should consider having some posters made too."

"For advertisements?"

Marigold nodded, and her dark auburn curls danced around her face. "That, and to sell as well. They won't cost much to produce. I know a guy who does printing. He might be agreeable to a deep discount since the proceeds are going to a good cause."

A chance to raise even more money for wildlife rescue? Things just kept getting better and better. And it was all thanks to Marigold pitching in. "You are really good at this, you know that?"

Was the redness creeping into Marigold's cheeks a blush? "I'm just part of the team. Your beer is the real star here."

They stood there for a moment, gazes locked but both silent. Kasma couldn't shake the feeling that, like her, Marigold was holding back, afraid to say something.

Finally Kasima found her voice again. "You said earlier you had some ideas for promotion that you wanted to discuss. Did you want to maybe get something to eat? We can talk it through over dinner?"

"Sure. In the taproom? I could go for a Cobb salad."

"I've been here at the brewery all day. How about I call up to the kitchen and order Cobb salads and a large order of fries to go. We can take them back to my place."

It was true, she was tired from a long day of work. But also, she wasn't thrilled with the idea of possibly running into her dad or Spencer while sharing yet another meal with Marigold. She still hadn't gotten around to telling them she and Marigold were no longer dating. She'd meant to—she didn't want to continue to lie to them. But any time the opportunity presented itself, all she could think about was the sad looks that would result when she told them she was her same old singleton self again. Not that she was sad to be single—that was still the way she preferred it—but she knew the way they would feel about it. No, a little privacy would be best. "I promise I have plenty of Enchanted Hops beer in my fridge at home."

Marigold laughed. "The famous Enchanted Hops craft beer? In that case, sure."

* * *

Marigold followed Kasima's Jeep for the fifteen-minute drive to her condo in Echo Park, a cute LA neighborhood with a trendy vibe. She parked on the street and met Kasima in her two-car garage. "Wow, you have lots of space here."

"Don't be fooled," Kasima said, leading her into her home. "It's tall and skinny. The space is an illusion. But it does have some perks."

Although the building didn't appear to be new construction, the unit was sleek and modern-looking. The decor was all clean lines and minimal frills, but the vibrant abstracts on the walls gave the place a classy pop of color. It was all perfectly Kasima.

After a quick stop in the galley-style kitchen to drop the food and Marigold's bag, Kasima led her up one set of stairs past the second floor and then another to show her what she meant by "perks." A small landing at the top of the staircase opened up to a private rooftop haven. A low, rectangular teak table was surrounded by a matching U-shaped sofa and chairs, and surrounding most of the rooftop oasis was large, potted greenery that gave the whole space a secret garden feel. The only break in the tall plants offered a view that included the Hollywood sign in the distance.

"This is a hell of a perk." Marigold took a deep breath as she surveyed the majestic sight. Savoring it. "How long have you lived here?"

"Almost ten years." Was that a hint of sadness that crossed her face? That didn't jibe with the pride that she'd been beaming with up to that point.

"Well, your home is beautiful," Marigold said as they headed back down the stairs to their salads. She was relieved to see the brightness return to Kasima's expression.

"Up on the roof is a great space to sit and have a beer, but not the best place for a meal. If you don't have to rush off, we could come back up after we eat."

Marigold instantly warmed at the idea of spending a little more time with her. "I'd love that."

Back inside they settled in at the dinette table adjacent to the galley kitchen. Maybe Kasima's condo wasn't huge, but it was furnished to make the most of the space. The colorful artwork that adorned the walls personalized the home. Marigold made a mental note to take a closer look at some of the pieces once they finished eating. But first, they had business to discuss.

"So, I have good news—I've booked you on a craft beer podcast for next week."

Kasima seemed to choke on her beer. "Me? On a podcast? People don't want to hear me talk about stuff. Maybe we could have Spencer do it. He's really the spokesperson of the brewery."

"You're the perfect person to do this," Marigold insisted. "You're the brewer. You came up with the recipe for Hooray For Howlywood. You have a passion for your work that really shines through when you talk about it. You're engaging and cool and beautiful—who wouldn't want to listen to you?" She had been focused on her salad while she said it, pushing the lettuce around to get the dressing more evenly distributed, but now that her gaze had lifted again she realized Kasima was staring at her with wide eyes.

She'd said "beautiful" out loud. And not in a "just friends" way.

She'd said too much. She'd become caught up in her feelings about Kasima and that "beautiful" had just slipped out. She'd blown right through the parameters of their original agreement and caught feelings, and now she'd basically said so out loud. She'd ruined everything.

Without a word Kasima got up from the table and walked to the big bay window on the far side of the room that looked out toward the city. Marigold's heart sunk. She hadn't meant to mess it all up. If friendship was all there could be between them, she would accept that. Maybe she could course correct. She joined Kasima and gazed out at the city that was just beginning to light up as the sun went down. *Just be honest.* She placed a hand on Kasima's shoulder and looked her in the eye. "I didn't mean to overstep. I'm sorry."

* * *

Kasima studied Marigold's face. So earnest in apology, almost pleading, when really there was no reason for her to be sorry.

Kasima's reaction was due to her body's response to Marigold's flattering words. The feeling had been building all the while they had been spending time together, and tonight when she noticed the heavy-lidded expression on Marigold's face while she spoke of passion and then called her beautiful—it had been a tipping point Kasima hadn't expected. Her core melted, but her heart soared. She'd stepped away not out of anger or annoyance, but rather to collect herself. A losing battle once she felt Marigold's touch on her shoulder and another wave of excitement washed over her. She'd been with other women in recent years—one nights stands, mostly—but she'd never brought any of them home to her house. Certainly not any women she considered kissable, anyway. But suddenly here with Marigold and this spark between them, it was too much to resist.

She held Marigold's gaze as she reached up and tucked a wayward auburn curl behind her ear, but then her focus slid down to those full, red lips and she was a goner. Her impulse surprised her probably as much as it did Marigold. "I'm going to kiss you now."

Marigold's eyes went wide, but she leaned in and suddenly their lips were centimeters apart. Millimeters. Kasima could smell the Hollywood Haze on her breath. Then finally it was happening. Their mouths crashed together, lips sliding, tongues tangling as the kiss deepened.

Kasima felt herself sinking into Marigold. Her hands tangled in those gorgeous dark-red curls. Marigold's touch was warm as she slid her fingertips under the hem of Kasima's T-shirt. The hard edges of what had been a busy day of work melted away. She surrendered to the delicious sensation of the hungry kiss and a desire was reignited inside her—one that she had forbade herself from expressing for so long. One that made her core pulse with want. Something real and solid that she didn't want to slip through her fingers but rather hold on to for dear life. She wanted nothing more than to kiss Marigold again and again. To give herself over to her.

Until they came up for air and she caught the image of Libby's artwork out of the corner of her eye. What the hell was she thinking? The kissing felt good now, but it could lead to heartbreak. She took a step back, desperate to put distance between them, and gasped for air, her head swimming in a sea of conflicting thoughts. Whether this was a result of the passionate kiss or because of the panic setting in she wasn't sure.

She registered the look of confusion on Marigold's face, but she couldn't find the words to smooth this over. All she knew was she had to retreat. She had to shut it all down. It didn't matter how attracted she was to Marigold or how much her body pulsed with the desire to get her upstairs and naked in her bed. She couldn't do this. She couldn't be intimate with Marigold and then walk it back to just being friends. And she couldn't start up a romantic relationship with her—she had no interest in putting her heart in a position to be shattered again. She wouldn't survive another hurt like that.

So it didn't matter how good the kiss felt, she had to stop it.

"I'm, uh...I'm so sorry," she stuttered as she tried to get control of her racing thoughts. "I just remembered I have to help my mom with something tonight. You're going to have to leave."

Marigold frowned, no doubt confused by this apparent one-eighty. "Kasima, did I do something wrong? Let's talk about this."

"It wasn't you. I just have to..." Her head was hot and dizzy, and she needed to be alone or at least not have this full-on internal battle in front of Marigold. It was so humiliating. "I'm late and I have to...Could you please just go? Please?"

"Yeah, okay." It was clear from her tone that Marigold wasn't okay with surrendering and leaving, but she grabbed her bag and walked to the door.

Kasima wished she could explain her behavior or at least be a little more polite, but tears were stinging the back of her eyes and the last thing she wanted was for Marigold to see her cry about this. Especially after... No, she wouldn't think about what had just happened between them. "I'll text you later."

"Sure," Marigold said as she walked out the door. She didn't look back as she left.

CHAPTER EIGHTEEN

Marigold started her Mini Cooper, but she didn't pull away from the curb right away. Instead, she sat and stared at Kasima's condo. What the hell just happened in there? One minute they had been tangled up in a scorching-hot kiss, and the next she was being shown the door on the basis of a fabrication. A really bad fabrication. Obviously Kasima didn't really have to rush off to her mom's house. Marigold had been sitting there for nearly eight minutes and Kasima hadn't come out yet.

"Help her mom with something, my ass," she muttered and turned the car's engine off again.

Why would Kasima lie to her and then kick her out? Was it because of the kiss? That didn't make any sense—Kasima was the one who started it. Not that Marigold hadn't thoroughly enjoyed it. She'd experienced steamy dreams focused on that exact scenario on more than one restless night recently. The way Kasima ran her fingers through her hair as they kissed and the hunger when she pushed her tongue past Marigold's lips—she had definitely been into it. It gave Marigold goose bumps just thinking about it. Yes, the kiss was very, very good. There had to be something she was missing, and she'd be damned if she was just going to drive off like a disappointed, slightly horny coward without an explanation. Without another thought, she got out of the Mini and marched back to the condo.

She wasn't completely surprised when Kasima didn't respond the first time she knocked on the door.

"Kasima, I know you didn't leave, and I'm a very persistent person," she said to the closed door. She was also a loud person; her voice carried. "I've got my tablet, and I will sit out here and work while I wait for you to give in and just answer the damn door. God knows I've got plenty of emails to catch up on."

When there was still no response, she sat down on the concrete slab in front of the door and dug through her tote bag, determined to make good on her threat. There was movement on the other side of the door—she could hear it.

"And I might sing too. I don't get nearly enough opportunity to show off the pipes the way I used too." She took a deep breath before belting out, "Morning has broken like the first morning. Blackbird has spoken like the first—"

"A hymn?" Kasima asked through the storm door. She had opened the heavy door and was now staring at Marigold through the glass pane with a mix of incredulity and amusement. "You're singing a hymn?"

"I surely am, although I always assume people first think of it as a Cat Stevens song before they go to hymn. To each their own, I suppose." Relief flooded through Marigold as she stood. She hadn't been completely certain Kasima would find any humor in the situation, being as upset as she clearly was when she kicked her out of the condo. Besides that, the hard cement had already proved an uncomfortable seat in those few minutes. "It was the first thing that popped into my head. But I do know all the verses if you want me to continue."

Kasima crossed her arms and blew out an exasperated sigh as if unsure of what to do with the dilemma Marigold was presenting on her doorstep.

"Blackbird has spoken—"

"Oh my God." Kasima opened the glass door. "Get in here before the neighbors start to wonder about the ruckus."

"You're comparing my singing voice to a ruckus?" She feigned offense. "I'll have you know that back in my child actor days, I was booked as a solid triple threat: acting, dancing, *and* singing." Her idea to keep the mood light did not seem to be working, but she stepped into the condo again, determined to figure out what the hell was going on.

"Why did you come back?" Kasima's expression was somber as she closed the door again.

"Why did you kick me out?" When Kasima dropped onto the sofa with her face in her hands instead of responding, Marigold sat beside her. "I'm not the one who pushed the boundaries of… whatever we're doing—friendship or partners in a marketing campaign. *You* kissed *me*."

"I know." Kasima's reply was muffled. "I wanted to kiss you."

"You wanted to kiss me, and I wanted to kiss you back, but for some reason, after the kiss happened you told me to leave." Marigold struggled to wrap her head around the situation. "And I want to know why. You owe me that much."

"Is that why you came back?" Kasima lowered her hands and met her gaze. There was something raw in her expression that hinted Marigold should tread lightly if she didn't want to risk expulsion again. "Because I *owe* you an explanation?"

Yeah, that was a poor choice of words. Kasima didn't owe her anything, and there was truly more than just the desire to share another kiss like that one behind Marigold's decision to knock on the door again. She could still picture the anguish that had been etched on Kasima's pretty face when she'd pleaded with her to leave. Something was wrong. And they could pretend that they were only spending time together because they were working on the campaign, but they had genuinely become friends along the way. She truly cared about Kasima, and despite the weird interaction between them earlier, she was willing to bet Kasima felt the same way about her.

"No, you don't owe me an explanation. I'm sorry I said that. But I'm your friend, and I care about you. I can see plainly that something's bothering you—that you're hurting—and my instinct is to try and make things better. Is there something that you want to talk about?"

Marigold had said her piece. She'd made the offer. Now she had to accept that might be all that she could do here. It was up to Kasima whether she wanted to open up to her about her concerns or not.

After a minute of angsty silence between them, Kasima finally nodded. She shifted on the sofa and tucked a leg under her so she was facing Marigold. Another deep breath. "I think I do owe you an explanation. It was a good kiss, and I liked it, but it can't happen again."

Marigold ran her tongue across her teeth, processing the words. The sentence didn't compute in her brain, but she could tell by the way Kasima stuck out her chin that she was certain of the words she'd spoken.

"Can you expand on that at all? If you liked the kiss, why wouldn't you want it to happen again?"

Kasima's cheeks pinked and the muscles in her jaw relaxed. "I didn't say I don't want…" She shook her head. "It can't happen again. I can't get involved in a romantic relationship. Because of that, all that would happen between us would be meaningless sex. And not that the sex wouldn't be hot and fun and exquisitely satisfying…" Her tongue flicked out to moisten her lips as if reflecting on the idea, but then she held up a hand as if coming to her senses again. "I like you. I like being friends with you. Plus, we're working on the campaign together and that could turn really awkward really fast."

"Nothing has to turn awkward," Marigold argued. She'd been waiting for an opportunity to broach the topic about giving dating a real try. It was time to shoot her shot. "Why do we have to be limited to meaningless sex? Maybe something real could develop between us—something wonderful."

"No." Kasima was adamant. "That's what I'm saying. It can't. I don't want that."

Marigold's stomach dropped. Kasima didn't want to get involved with her and that was that. It was a sucker punch to the gut, but least she had been clear about how she felt and not strung her along. *Talk about things turning awkward. Yikes!* Why did she have to go and press the issue?

She pushed up from the sofa. "I, uh, I guess I'll go then. Sorry about…all this." Grabbing her tote once more, she strode to the door. The same exit she'd made earlier. She should never have come back after the first time. She should have respected Kasima's need to be alone.

"I'm a widow." Kasima's voice was so soft Marigold wasn't sure she'd heard her correctly.

She stopped with her hand literally on the doorknob. All of her embarrassment and all of her hurt feelings dropped away. When she turned around, it was a watery-eyed Kasima standing there. Her heart went out to her. The pat phrases people normally uttered under these circumstances felt woefully anemic, but still she automatically said, "I'm sorry."

"It was five years ago. My wife, Libby, was in a car accident. She died in the ambulance on the way to the hospital. She was gone. Just like that. I never even got to say goodbye." Kasima briefly closed her eyes. It almost appeared as if she was relieved to finally tell Marigold the truth, as painful as that truth may have been for her. "We weren't even thirty years old. We'd just celebrated our fifth wedding anniversary the week before. Fancy, champagne-soaked dinner at Spago. And then she was gone. My heart was gone."

"I had no idea. I don't even know what to say. I'm just so very sorry," Marigold said. She reached to put a comforting hand on Kasima's shoulder, but she stepped out of range.

"Thank you. But I'm not telling you this so you'll feel sorry for me." The hard resolution was back in Kasima's eyes. "I'm telling you so you'll understand. I never want to go through a loss like that again. I can't. It took me months after Libby's death before I could even function again. I just…I didn't feel like myself anymore and it took a damn long time before I even had a glimmer of that sensation again. My parents were so worried. They still are. That's why they're always on my case to be social, get out and meet people. They're just trying to help. But I'm just not willing to risk losing someone I care about like that again."

Marigold finally understood. "You're avoiding the risk of loss by avoiding relationships altogether."

Kasima nodded. "Like I said, I really do like you, and I value the friendship we've developed. I don't want to mess that up."

They had come a long way since that fake date at the fundraiser. And Marigold enjoyed spending time with Kasima. Was she attracted to her in a more than friends way? For sure. Was having a friendship with Kasima better than having no relationship with her at all? Definitely.

Marigold took a cleansing breath and made up her mind. "I value our friendship too. So, maybe we can pretend like that kiss never happened and just kind of...hit the reset button on our friendship?"

"You're really okay with that? I mean, I know it probably seems weird, but I've made my decision about this. I can't risk that kind of loss again. I—"

"You don't have to say anything else." Marigold shook her head. She'd made her decision too. "I'm happy just to be friends with you."

And despite the ache in her heart, she mostly meant it.

CHAPTER NINETEEN

Kasima sat holed up in the taproom manager's office, deep breathing along to the mindfulness app on her phone. The *Beer With Me* podcast crew of two had been setting up in the taproom for the past thirty minutes, and she'd managed to ignore them for most of that time. But as the minutes ticked down to go time, her anxiety had ramped up, and she'd retreated to the little office off of the kitchen. Why did she ever let Marigold talk her into this? She didn't know what she was supposed to say to these folks. She was a behind-the-scenes woman, not a spokesperson. Maybe it wasn't too late to back out. She fired off a quick text to Marigold.

Changed my mind—can't do this. I'll get Spence to come out and talk to them.

Three bubbles immediately appeared on her screen to indicate an incoming text, but they disappeared just as quickly. It didn't matter. There was nothing Marigold could text that would make her go out there. Being on a podcast was beyond her comfort zone. She was out of her depth. She wasn't going to do it. They didn't do any of these types of publicity stunts the last time they did the SoCal Wildlife Rescue special release and it did just fine. She was about to hit send on her SOS text to her brother when her zen from the mindfulness app was shattered by three sharp raps on the office door.

"Don't you dare pass the buck to Spencer. You're the person we need on this podcast. I don't know how many times I can tell you that." Marigold's voice was muffled by the heavy door, but her message was clear. She wasn't letting Kasima duck out of the podcast. Before Kasima could work up a good argument, Marigold was pounding on the door again. "You are not going to chicken out on me. Open this door. Let's go."

Kasima felt the rush of adrenaline release in her system, but this time it wasn't due to her nervousness about the podcast. It was Marigold's commanding presence. Stern Marigold was a mighty attractive Marigold. *Wait. Stop that.* She shook her head to clear it. She wasn't having those kinds of feelings about Marigold—especially not in this moment. How inappropriate could she get? This was just the adrenaline messing with her. Despite her potential fears, Kasima opened the door and stepped out of the office.

"I can't do this." Kasima shook her head. "I don't know anything about podcasts."

"Then I guess it's a good thing they're not here to talk about podcasts with you." Marigold put her hands on Kasima's shoulders and marched her out of the office. "You do know a hell of a lot about beer. That's what you're going to talk about."

They continued moving through the kitchen and back into the taproom. Any relief Kasima had felt at the appearance of stern Marigold and her grasp on her shoulders evaporated at the sight of the podcast equipment set up at the booth in the back corner of the room. Her throat tightened a little more with each step they took. "Are you sure this is such a good idea? My dad is probably on the campus somewhere. He'd be great at this sort of thing."

"I don't want Spence to do this, and I don't want your dad. I want you." Marigold's cheeks went pink, and her eyes went wide. "I mean, I want you to do the podcast. You're the perfect person to talk about Hooray For Howlywood because you're the one who has seen it through from concept to final product. You're the one at the heart of this project, Kasima, and I think people will really connect with what you have to say."

There was a sparkle of confidence in Marigold's eyes that made the pinch between Kasima's shoulders release a fraction. Did her deep-green eyes always have that bright golden hue shining around the edges? She didn't remember noticing just how beautiful they were before.

Marigold seemed to be certain she could handle this. Maybe she should have a little more faith in herself.

Kasima stopped one of the servers who was heading toward the bar. "When you get a second, would you please bring two glasses of Hooray For Howlywood to that booth?" She nodded to the podcast corner. She had another thought. "And bring an unopened set of all four cans. We may as well get the 'collect them all' message out there too."

"Now you're talking like a marketer." Marigold smiled that Hollywood smile at her, and a traitorous flutter of excitement that had nothing to do with the podcast erupted in Kasima's belly.

She still had no idea what she was going to say on the podcast, but she gave a brave, stiff nod to Marigold and took her seat at the table.

Rick, the host of the *Beer With Me* podcast, was an affable guy with a deep, upbeat voice. He greeted her with a hearty handshake before launching into a rundown of what the plan was for the next thirty minutes or so that they would spend recording. It sounded simple enough—he had some questions that he typically asked guests of the show, then she would have a chance to talk specifically about Hooray For Howlywood. At the very end they would play a game that was a beer-centric version of This or That. His calm demeanor eased some of her apprehension even as Matt, the other guy on the podcast crew, adjusted the microphone in front of her.

"If you're ready, we'll begin," Rick said with a kind smile.

"Lez ride." That she borrowed the ridiculous catchphrase of Dakota Oakley was indicative of just how potent her case of nerves was, friendly host or not. She caught the raised eyebrow

Marigold threw her way but tried to ignore it as Rick launched into his standard introduction for *Beer With Me*. She swiped the back of her hand across her hairline. Was it especially hot in the taproom today or something?

"I'm at Enchanted Hops Brewing Company with Kasima Powell, who is the brewmaster here at her family's brewery. Kasima, tell us a little bit about your role here."

She leaned in close to the microphone. "I'm the head brewer here at Enchanted Hops." *No kidding*, she admonished herself. *He just said that.* She saw Marigold off to the side nodding encouragingly for her to go on. "As such, I oversee all brewing processes on site and I'm ultimately responsible for the quality of our product."

As such? What the hell was that? God, she was making a job she loved sound so spectacularly dull. What was that expression on Marigold's face? Was she trying not to cringe?

"But I also get to create new beers, which is fun," Kasima added, noting Marigold's frantic gestures imploring her to say more. "And it is very cool."

"I couldn't agree more. Beer is fun and very cool," Rick laughed. The host with the most. "Maybe you could tell us a little more about where you find inspiration for the new beers you create."

Kasima nodded to buy herself a little time while she took a swallow of beer to calm her nerves, then she realized how stupid that was considering listeners of the podcast would not see her nodding or reacting at all to Rick. Why did it feel like all of the blood had rushed out of her brain, leaving her high and dry in the common sense department? She opened her mouth to respond verbally this time, but she must have swallowed the beer a little too quickly because—to her horror—she belched right into the microphone.

Rick's jovial laugh rang in her ears, and she immediately clapped her hands firmly over her mouth to stop herself from emitting any more sounds—including words. Screw this whole podcast promotion. She tried and she failed. She was done.

Her face burned with embarrassment as she turned her gaze to Marigold, silently pleading for her to pull the plug on the podcast and put her out of her misery.

Marigold whispered something to Matt before raising her hand and approaching the table. "Okay, can we just…can we cut?" She didn't appear bothered by Rick's questioning look as she pushed her way onto the booth bench next to him. Her voice was stern again as she locked eyes with Kasima. "What exactly is happening here?"

"Oh, not much," Kasima deadpanned. "Just a little self-humiliation being recorded for public consumption."

"All right, you can stop the pity party," Marigold chastised her. "Take a beat and take a breath, and we'll get ready to go again."

"I'm ready whenever you are," Rick offered, before taking a drink of his beer and nodding approval. "This is good stuff."

Go again? Did they not just hear that disaster of an effort?

"No." Kasima shook her head adamantly. "We're done here. I'm sorry, Rick, your podcast is great, but obviously I'm not good at this. Your listeners deserve better."

"My listeners are like me—we're beer lovers." Rick's voice was full of sincerity—all traces of laughter gone. "Believe me, they're going to want to hear about your family's brewery and the person behind Hooray For Howlywood. And then they're going to go out and buy your beer. Because it's a damn good brew."

"Thank you for that, but I literally just belched into the microphone, and my answers before that couldn't have sounded much better."

Marigold reached across the table and grabbed her hand. Despite Kasima's prickly mood, the soft touch was a comfort. "You're not wrong. You were really stinking it up."

"God, don't sugarcoat it." Was that her idea of helping? Kasima tried to pull her hand away, but Marigold wasn't letting go.

"Let me finish." Marigold's expression softened. "You started off pretty rough, but Rick and Matt can edit that out."

"Edit it out?"

"Oh sure, you kidding me? We edit the whole thing before we post it." Rick waved a dismissive hand in the air. "You think we haven't heard a burp before? Me and the folks I have on the show consume plenty of beer while we're recording. Matt has a whole blooper reel of people burping."

"Hell, you should hear the one of people letting a toot from the boot rip," Matt piped up from behind his laptop.

Kasima still had her doubts. They could edit out any bodily outbursts she may let slip, but she still needed to give some kind of coherent response to Rick's questions, and thus far she'd fallen flat on that front. "I don't know. I'm still not sure I have anything to say that people will want to hear."

"Sweetie," Marigold said, giving her hand a fortifying squeeze. "Just say it to me for some practice." She glanced over at Rick as if asking for approval, and he returned a "why not" shrug. "Tell me how you got started in this business. You know, what made you want to be a brewmaster?"

Kasima stubbornly clamped her mouth shut and fixed her with a hard stare, still not convinced this was a good idea. She'd made enough of a fool of herself for one day already.

"You want to raise as much money for the wildlife rescue as you can, right?" Marigold leaned back in her seat and met her challenging look. Apparently, she could be stubborn as well. "You've got to at least try. Just practice. Tell me the story."

Kasima took a deep breath. Marigold was right. She did want to do right by SoCal Wildlife Rescue. And this was just telling the story to Marigold. If the tale sucked, it would just prove the point she was trying to make in the first place—that she wasn't cut out to be any type of spokesperson—and she could just call the whole podcast thing off.

"As you know," she began tentatively, "my dad started Enchanted Hops Brewing Company in 2001. I had just turned eleven. Back then we had a brewery only—the taproom didn't open until 2015. Some Saturdays when my dad had to come out here, he would bring me along with him, and I just…I loved the science of it all."

"You mean the process of making beer?" Marigold asked. "Like, the chemical reactions and all of that?"

"Not exactly," Kasima admitted. "When I was a kid, I used to love coming to the brewery and hanging out in the fermentation tank room. I loved to pretend the tanks were spaceships, and I was part of a top-secret mission to explore outer space. I would run through the tank room shouting instructions to my make-believe staff of astronauts, and then of course, counting down to takeoff."

When Marigold laughed out loud at this revelation, Kasima joined in, and with that, the vise grip that had taken hold in her chest since Rick and Matt arrived at the taproom released. The longer they discussed Kasima's path to becoming head brewer—from working part-time at the brewery when she was in high school scrubbing tanks and doing other grunt work to majoring in chemistry at Pomona College to working as a production brewer at Enchanted Hops until she had enough experience to earn her current position—the more she relaxed.

She then told Marigold and Rick the story of how her father paired up their brewery with SoCal Wildlife Rescue and how once she became head brewer she came up with the idea to brew an annual special release with the proceeds going to the organization. It had taken her a couple of years to make it happen, but now they were releasing their second special brew. From that point, it felt natural for her to talk about the West Coast IPA she'd created for this year's release, including the fact that there were four different cans for collecting.

"Well, I've learned a few things about you today." Marigold beamed at her. "And you've made it quite clear how much you love your job."

"No one would do this job if they didn't love it." Kasima shrugged. "Brewing craft beer isn't just a job. It's really more of a lifestyle."

Rick pointed a finger at her. "Now, that's a fantastic sound bite."

"Yeah," Kasima agreed feeling lighter than she had all day. "I think I'm ready to record now."

"Matt, what do you think?" Rick looked to his counterpart, who was still sitting behind his laptop.

"We don't need anything else." He gave a thumbs-up.

Kasima's heart sunk. Had she blown this chance to promote Hooray For Howlywood and SoCal Wildlife Rescue with her blundering responses to Rick's questions at the beginning of this whole thing? Now that she finally felt comfortable enough to be recorded, they were going to call it off?

"I don't understand. Have you decided not to feature Enchanted Hops after all?"

"Oh, we're featuring you," Rick reassured her. "But we can take the last twenty minutes of conversation we had here, edit in me asking the questions instead of Marigold, and put together the whole Q and A portion of the podcast. All we need to do now is record the This or That segment, and we're good to go."

Kasima shook her head. "I still don't understand. What conversation are you talking about?"

Marigold's smile was triumphant. "I asked Matt to keep recording while I sat down to talk to you. I've seen your passion when talking about craft beer before. I knew if we could just get you going you would shine, and you sure did. You were wonderful. Congratulations."

There was something infectious in the gleam of pride in Marigold's eyes that bolstered Kasima's confidence tenfold. She could be a spokesperson for Enchanted Hops if she wanted to. Nobody else but her dad knew the ins-and-outs of the brewery and their products as intimately as she did. She just needed a little reminder, and that was exactly what Marigold had given her. As she looked into Mari's forest-green eyes, a different sensation suddenly erupted in her chest—desire.

"What do you think?" Rick broke the spell. "Ready to play This or That: Beer Edition?"

"On one condition." Kasima shared a playful grin. "Can I get a do-over on that introduction? Maybe without the burp this time?"

CHAPTER TWENTY

Sunday evening Marigold was in Kasima's office at the brewery again going over plans for the release event, this time to unveil the posters she'd had made with Kasima's label designs. The original sketches were beautiful in their own right, but the colorful images of the owl, mountain lion, opossum, and black bear blown up into movie-poster size were absolutely striking. Kasima had actually gasped when the first one had been unfurled, and that made Marigold's heart happy.

"I love each one more than the next," Kasima gushed.

"I know. Me too," Marigold agreed. "You did an amazing job on them." She hesitated for a moment—wanting to be respectful yet too curious to resist—before asking a question that had been on her mind for a while. "The vibrant colors and bold strokes remind me of the artwork you have on your walls at home. Was that what you were going for?"

Kasima nodded, but a hint of sadness flashed in her eyes even as she smiled. "Those paintings were done by my wife. Libby was an artist by both trade and passion. When she was working on a piece, she poured her entire self into it. I think that's reflected in the results. She'd done a few art shows at local galleries in the time we were together, and she did very well at them. I think eventually she would've become very successful. God knows there was no stopping that woman once she put her mind to something."

"No doubt," Marigold said softly, ignoring the ding of an incoming text on her phone. "I think she would be very proud of your label designs."

"Thank you for saying that." Kasima gave her upper arm a gentle squeeze. "Libby was talented, kind, and unapologetically silly when the moment struck. Just an incredible woman. I was lucky to have her in my life. I aim to carry a little bit of her light with me in the way I move through life."

Marigold thought back on the past few weeks. Kasima definitely ticked the talented and kind boxes on that list. Suddenly images of Kasima zipping around the roller rink in her pink glittery skates flashed in her mind, and she had to stifle a laugh. Yep, third box ticked as well. "I would say you totally do."

"That's all I can hope for." Kasima beamed. Any trace of sadness was gone from her eyes, replaced by something that looked a lot like pride. Marigold was relieved that her inquiry had been well received and that Kasima had trusted her enough to share this insight with her.

The moment was interrupted when her phone chirped with another text, followed by one more right after that.

"You should check that." Kasima nodded in the direction of the ignored phone.

"That's Elle's text tone. I can catch up with her later."

But when the phone chirped again and Kasima shot her a pointed look, she checked the message—a picture of Ava wearing a cowboy hat riding a mechanical bull, beer bottle in hand, with the caption: *Isn't this your girl?*

Marigold groaned as her eyes scanned the screen and read the follow-up text.

At Tequila On Sunset. You might want to collect your charge. She's drawing attention. Not the good kind.

"Crap," Marigold muttered as she poked at her phone to call Elle.

Behind her desk, Kasima stood, her eyes full of concern. "What is it?"

Marigold rolled her eyes, hoping to convey the call was not a matter of life or death, merely annoying ridiculousness. Into her phone she said, "What's going on?"

The other end of the connection was full of rowdy bar crowd noise as Elle responded. "The situation here is taking a turn. Seems Ava hit on the wrong woman—a woman whose actual fiancée is less than pleased about the situation. Ava is not backing down." The muffled shouting in the background got louder, as if Elle was getting closer to the source. "Aaaaaand the fiancée just discovered Ava is underage."

Nothing good could come from an angry woman shouting in public about an inebriated Ava Ashford being underage. Now that she knew about what was going on, Marigold had no choice but to try to extract her client from the situation. Allison would have a fit if she knew she had been tipped off and still left Ava to twist in the wind. Or buck on the bronco, as the case may be.

"I'm on my way."

As she clicked off the call, she could only imagine what Kasima would think of her running out when they were in the middle of a planning session for the campaign. It certainly wasn't very professional of her. But managing Ava's career was her job, and the beer stuff was just...well, it was fun. Fun time was over—her job was calling. When she faced Kasima again, she didn't see anger or jealousy in her expression. All she saw was concern.

"Is the kid okay?"

"She might not be once I get my hands on her," Marigold grumbled as she collected her things. "I'm sorry about cutting our meeting short."

"Don't worry about it." Kasima shook her head. "I can take it from here. Go save the day and we'll talk later."

Twelve minutes later, Marigold was approaching the entrance to Tequila On Sunset, but she was too late. Ava was being put into the back of a LAPD squad car.

"Marigold!" Ava screeched drunkenly when she spotted her. "This is so bogus. I didn't do anything."

That was unlikely. She approached the car, hoping to not have to shout back in response, but the police officers warned her to stay back. There was nothing she could do to stop them from taking Ava to the station. She would have to move on to plan B. "Don't say anything else. I'll call your attorney and meet you at the police station," she called back, hoping that Ava could hear her through the car door. Then she ducked into Tequila On Sunset to look for Elle.

She found her sitting next to Ashley at a long cocktail table full of hunky guys and stick-thin women. Definite Hollywood types.

"Tequila On Sunset?" Marigold asked Elle as she bellied up to the table. "Trying something new?"

"It's Ashley's ex's birthday party," Elle replied with a nod in the direction of one of the guys Marigold recognized as David Carlson.

"And they're having the celebration here at"—she checked her watch—"seven thirty?"

"Please." Elle rolled her eyes. "This is merely the preparty. These action movie hero types go hard. In a couple hours we'll move to the actual party venue."

It sounded like Elle was in for an even longer night than she was. "Better you than me. I don't think I could keep up with that kind of pace anymore. Definitely not on a Sunday night."

"Believe me, I'll pay for it tomorrow. But for today I'll live like a rock star. Or action hero at least," Elle said before signaling to the server for another drink. "You want anything?"

Marigold shook her head. "I'm going to be in enough trouble with my boss when this all shakes out without adding drinking on the job to the list of my transgressions. Just tell me what you saw here so I can make a plan to spin it."

Elle quickly relayed the events of the afternoon. Ava had already been at the establishment when David's party arrived. Elle had spotted her at the bar but didn't pay her much attention until about an hour later when she'd snapped that picture of Ava on the mechanical bull. Ava was putting on quite a show for the other patrons, hooting and hollering, and repeatedly spouting her catchphrase, "Lez ride!"

"I am really starting to hate those words."

"I can imagine." Elle nodded sympathetically before continuing her story. "Things really went south for Ava when she started making moves on one of the women who had been watching her ride the bull and basically egging her on."

Elle went on to describe the exchange that quickly went from Ava flirting with an apparent fan, to full-press, up-close hitting on her which included especially handsy caressing and heads together whispering. It was no surprise when the fan's fiancée finally showed up and was very much not a fan of what was happening.

"A shouting match ensued, and the bouncer came over and broke it up," Elle explained. "I thought that would be it, but I guess the fiancée wasn't over it, because the next thing I knew she was shouting again and making a big deal about Ava being underage. You can probably thank Google for that. Then the cops showed up."

"I can pick the thread up from there." Marigold sighed. What a mess. She should be hanging out with Kasima, not spending the night springing her client from the pokey. "I guess I better get down to the police station and see about bailing her out. This kid is going to be the death of me."

"Orrr…" Elle began in a cautious tone, but she should have just spit it out—Marigold knew exactly what was coming. "You could give Ava some tough love. Let her stew in a cell overnight. Tell her with some force that if she wants to be successful long term she needs to straighten up and fly right."

Elle didn't get it. She only knew the client's point of view on the subject, not the part where you had a firm pulling the strings behind the scenes and calling the shots. Marigold was more of a middleman in this situation. Elle's heart was in the right place, but the reality was Marigold had to do what the higher-ups demanded. In this case, that was keeping Ava happy and reacting with damage control as her whims dictated.

"I wish." Marigold stood. Now that she had the scoop it was time to get back to work. "But Allison has other plans for this particular client's management. Anyway, thanks for the help. I'll call you later."

After leaving the bar and making contact with Ava's personal attorney, Marigold drove directly to the station where they took Ava for processing, hoping she'd given the officers enough time to complete whatever it was they had to do. She needn't have worried—by the time she walked into the West Hollywood Community Station, Ava was sitting at the desk of a middle-aged female officer who looked more captivated by the young star than interested in prosecuting her for public intoxication. Ava seemed to be charming the pants off this woman. *Of course she was.*

"I'm being completely serious." Ava's voice was definitely in flirtation register, and she leaned so far forward as she gazed back at the officer that there was a real threat of her chest just popping right out of the unnecessarily low V-neck of her threadbare white shirt. Thank heavens it hadn't been wet T-shirt contest night at Tequila On Sunset—Ava would've no doubt been a contender for first place in that get-up. "It said on my resume that I knew how to ride a horse, but I never actually did it until the first day I showed up on the set."

"Oh, you are trouble, aren't you?" The officer—who had to be old enough to be Ava's mother—had the audacity to actually bat her eyelashes as she teased her.

"I guess some people think so," Ava said with an exaggerated wink. "But really, I'm harmless."

It was time to rein in this twisted version of the *Bachelorette*.

"Sorry to interrupt." Marigold waved her hand as she approached the desk.

"Ma'am, you're not supposed to come back here." The officer stood, as if ready to jump into action at this infraction of the rules. Where was that fun, flirty tone now?

"There was nobody at the desk out front, and I could see my client—"

"Ma'am." Apparently, the officer wasn't quite as charmed by Marigold as she was Ava. "Please return to the lobby. And somebody will be right with you."

"It's okay, Janice." Ava sounded absolutely giddy with the turn of events. "She's with me."

Janice? Ava is on a first name basis with the local police force now?

"Oh, well, that's fine then." The officer—Janice—sat back down, but she continued to scowl in her direction. "You the attorney?"

"No, but he's on his way." Marigold took a protective step closer to Ava, who was sitting crisscross applesauce style in the wooden chair adjacent to Officer Janice's desk. Perfectly comfortable hanging out in the police station.

There was a strained beat of silence before Janice spoke again. "I don't think that's going to be necessary. I think we can let Miss Ashford go with just a warning this time. The manager of Tequila On Sunset doesn't want to take any action, and Ava has promised me she won't get into this sort of trouble again."

Ava's expression was a mask of saccharine-sweet innocence as her gaze bounced from Janice to Marigold. Funny how Marigold had heard that same promise from Ava a few times now, and yet here they were in the West Hollywood Community Police Station. *Whatever.* At least they were getting out of there with nothing on Ava's record.

"Thank you, Janice," Ava gushed. "I really do promise."

"Let me just go wrap up some paperwork on this and we'll have you out of here in a jiffy," Janice said as she rose from her seat, the scowl gone now that her attention was back on the young star. Before she walked away, she put a hand on Ava's shoulder. "Of course, you still owe me that selfie with me before you go."

Ava put a hand over her heart. "Of course."

It was nearly one hour later by the time everything was signed off on and the promised selfie was snapped. Finally, Marigold had Ava in her car en route to the house she shared with her grandmother.

She wanted to say something wise to the younger woman—some long-haul career advice about image and public perception, but she couldn't get Allison's "kid gloves" warning out of her head. At the very least she wanted confirmation that Ava's adventures were over for the night and that she would sober up in the safe space of her grandmother's home. "Please tell me this concludes your activities for the evening. You smell like a distillery. Just call it a night and sleep it off, okay? You got really lucky tonight. You know that, right?"

"My fans love me, what can I say?" She was so fucking smug.

"I'm serious." Marigold didn't try to hide her frustration this time.

Ava crossed her arms and stared ahead in sullen silence as the car rolled to a stop in front of the house.

"Do you need me to stay with you while you sober up?" Marigold shifted in her seat to try to catch Ava's gaze. Why was she being so damn stubborn?

"No."

When Ava unbuckled her seat belt, Marigold did the same.

"What are you doing?" Ava looked appalled.

"I'm just going to come in and say hello to your grandmother."

"No," Ava said quickly. "I don't need you to tattle on me to my grandma. I swear, I won't go anywhere else tonight."

Marigold shook her head slowly. "Ava, I'm not trying to tattle on you. I just haven't seen your grandmother in a while, and I'd like to say hello."

"She's probably already in bed."

Marigold glanced at her watch. "It's just a little after nine."

"She's old. She goes to bed early."

It was obvious to Marigold that Ava was lying about something, but why would she keep her from speaking with her grandmother? It wasn't worth the hassle of arguing, she decided. She could imagine Allison's disapproval if either Ava or her grandmother complained about her insisting on entering their home at a late hour. She blew out a sigh of surrender. "Okay, Ava. Get a good night's sleep. Drink some water before you go to bed. And no more alcohol tonight."

"Okay, okay. I hear you," Ava said as she climbed out of the passenger side. "Thanks for the ride."

Better than no thanks at all, Marigold thought.

Without a backward glance, Ava disappeared into the dark house. A light flicked on in one of the front rooms and Marigold pulled away from the curb. She still couldn't shake the feeling that something wasn't quite right. The quiet residential road was empty, so she made a U-turn and parked on the opposite side of the street, a few houses down from Ava's. She sat there for twenty minutes answering emails and reading an article about the recent promotional success of a family-run craft brewery in Chicago while the house remained still with Ava safely inside.

She was the one being ridiculous now. The fact was, Ava was a grown woman and had every right to come and go as she pleased. There was no legitimate reason for Marigold to sit there any longer like some kind of glorified babysitter. She started the car and headed home.

CHAPTER TWENTY-ONE

Marigold ambled through her house with a zip hoodie thrown over her camisole pajama set, totally worn out from her Ava Ashford rescue mission. It felt like ages ago that she had been at Enchanted Hops planning the release party with Kasima. Now the only thing she was planning was a cup of chamomile tea and a fuzzy blanket to curl up in. It was after ten thirty and her bed was practically calling out to her by name.

She was home for less than twenty minutes when the doorbell rang. She tipped her head from side to side trying to lessen the stiffness in her neck. If that was Ava Ashford at her door, she was going to lose it. A quick peek at the doorbell camera on her phone revealed it was not the starlet. Instead, Kasima stood on her porch hoisting a large tote bag over her shoulder and a brown paper grocery sack in her arms.

"What the hell?" she muttered as she rushed to the door to help with the parcels. "Kasima, I'm happy to see you, but it's been a long day. I'm terrible company, I'm sure. What is all this stuff and what are you doing here?"

Kasima handed off one of the bags as she walked through the doorway, completely ignoring Marigold's hints that she wasn't up to a visit.

"I'm guessing you haven't eaten anything because you were too busy saving your client from self-destruction and you forgot," Kasima called over her shoulder as she continued to march straight to the kitchen and began emptying the contents of her tote bag onto the island countertop.

Marigold followed behind and set her bag on the counter as well, eying skeptically the items Kasima was unloading. Cheese, whole milk, butter, spices. The events of the evening had set her on edge and bolstered her annoyance at Kasima's completely correct assessment of her failure to eat dinner. "You didn't have to do all this." She gestured to the groceries, still unsure what Kasima had up her sleeve. "Whatever this is."

"Why don't you have a seat and let me unpack this." Kasima grabbed the second sack of supplies and pulled out several takeout containers from Enchanted Hops. "Don't worry, I brought us salads to balance out the meal, but it's not really about that. It's more about comfort. I'm making you one of my favorite comfort foods." The last item she pulled out of the bag was a six-pack of beer cans.

"Do you really think it's a good idea for us to split a six-pack at this time of night when we both have to be at work in the morning?"

"Tonight we're not drinking. We're eating," Kasima said with a smart grin as she plucked one can from the bunch and stashed the others in the refrigerator. She clicked on the oven before turning back to Marigold. "Do you have a saucepan I can use?"

"Bottom cabinet, right there by the stove," Marigold instructed from her seat at the island. She was too tired to fight it, but if Kasima was going to insist on this intrusion, she could do the work.

Kasima located the pan and started combining ingredients, pausing only to pour and set a tall glass of water in front of Marigold. "Drink this. I'm guessing you haven't hydrated properly all evening either. And start on your salad."

Apparently it was Bossy Kasima who had showed up. Marigold didn't totally mind. It was a relief to have someone else be in charge for a change. "I don't want to start without you."

"Don't be silly." Kasima continued to whisk flour into the melted butter in the saucepan. "I ate my dinner already. I only brought salad for myself to keep you company. But I will one hundred percent be partaking of the beer cheese."

"Beer cheese?" Her stomach growled in anticipation as she watched Kasima add the milk to the pan.

"Mmm hmm. To go with these." Kasima stopped whisking long enough to put the taproom's house-made pretzel sticks she'd brought on a baking sheet and pop them in the oven. "I promise you—it's the ultimate comfort food. Now, tell me how things went with Ava."

"Ugh." Marigold put her head in her hands. "She's a complete dumpster fire" seemed like a real bummer of a statement and a harsh thing to say about a client, even if it was deserved. She didn't want to bitch about work while Kasima was being so kind to her. "You don't want to hear my sad work story."

"Are you kidding?" Kasima grinned over her shoulder as she added Worcestershire sauce, Dijon mustard, and garlic powder to the melting cheese. "And miss out on the latest Ava Ashford scoop? No, I'm totally here for it."

She shot her a withering look. One of the key components of successfully spinning poor client behavior was not going around blabbing about said client's behavior. She was a professional secret keeper. It had been a point of contention in relationships with past partners who felt she was reluctant to open up with them. But damn, it would feel good to debrief and vent. Kasima had been vulnerable and honest when telling her about Libby. She was trustworthy.

"If I say anything—and I'm not saying I will—you have to swear you will vault it."

Over her shoulder, Kasima mimed zipping her lips before returning to her food prep.

While Kasima plated the soft pretzel sticks and ladled the cheese sauce into a crock, Marigold relayed the events of her evening, including how she sat in the car observing the house like some kind of celebrity stalker to make sure Ava didn't leave again.

"It sounds like this girl is a real…" Kasima widened her eyes to indicate her alarm. "Piece of work. What a way to spend your night."

"It's all part of the job for me. I mean, I can understand. I've been there," Marigold said with a shrug. "Young and on your own trying to navigate the business and trappings of sudden fame. Even if it was somewhat fleeting in my case. Ava has her grandmother looking out for her, but I'm not sure how much Ava listens to her advice when it comes to her social life. There's a lot of temptation and pitfalls out there."

"You managed to avoid them."

Marigold grabbed napkins out of the holder for each of them. "I'm not going to say there weren't a few missteps along the way, but I guess for the most part I was lucky." The spicy aroma of the cheese hit and Marigold's mouth instantly began to water. Time to pivot from the subject of work and get to the food. "And now I'm super lucky because you made me beer cheese."

"Certainly sounds like you've earned this tonight." Kasima joined her at the island counter with the food.

"That looks delicious." Marigold pushed her unfinished salad out of the way and reached for a pretzel. Veggies had nothing on carbs when it came to comfort.

"Careful—that's basically molten cheese. Hot stuff." The playful wink that accompanied Kasima's words made Marigold's stomach flutter.

Despite the warning, Marigold broke off a piece of pretzel and dipped it into the creamy golden cheese. A whisper of steam released as she swirled it in the crock, so instead of popping it directly into her mouth as she'd originally planned, she patiently set the bite on her plate to cool for a moment. "Not gonna lie, this is hard to resist." She was referring mostly to the snack. Only a little bit to the woman sitting beside her.

"Trust me, it's worth the wait." Kasima winked and dipped her pretzel into the cheese. "I used The Hops Father, which is our current Bavarian IPA. I chose it because the slight bitterness and citrusy notes pair well with the cheddar." That passion for all things beer was shining in her eyes again. As tired as Marigold felt after her celebrity rescue mission, Kasima's contagious enthusiasm gave her a surge of energy. "I know, I'm rambling on about beer again, but here's the thing…"

She could have kept rambling on about beer all night as far as Marigold was concerned, even after the exhausting evening she'd experienced. She found it hard to tear her gaze away from those gorgeous brown eyes. "What?"

"While I was talking, the cheese cooled off enough for us to eat it."

"Thank God," Marigold said quickly before popping the cheese-covered piece of soft pretzel in her mouth. The combination of the spices in the beer and the sharpness of the cheddar made her taste buds tingle, and the warmth of the bite did exactly as Kasima promised—provided waves of comfort. She had to admit, Kasima's unexpected visit along with the food had been exactly what was needed to turn her mood around. A moan escaped her lips as she reached for another piece.

"Good, isn't it?" Kasima beamed.

"Good? Nah." Marigold shook her head. "This is orgasmic. No, it might be better than sex."

Kasima's laugh had a sarcastic edge to it. "That's a whole other level of comfort, but don't look at me—I wouldn't really know. I haven't had sex in about eight months."

The confession startled Marigold, and for a moment she wondered if she'd made a mistake by even referring to sex, but when Kasima shifted her expression to an exaggerated version of Melpomene, the mask of tragedy, she relaxed and laughed along with her.

That was when the idea began to take hold in her mind. Kasima had provided her much-needed comfort in the form of food. Why couldn't she—strictly as a friend—show Kasima some comfort with sex?

She grabbed Kasima's hand and gave it a squeeze. "Thank you for doing this for me. I didn't know how badly I needed it."

"You're welcome."

Marigold shifted in her seat, working up the courage to say the next part. "And I think you should stay tonight. Stay here with me."

Kasima's eyes flashed gold, but then her expression sobered and her spine appeared to stiffen. Her posture was rigid—like she was on high alert. "Marigold, I told you I don't want a relationship. Nothing's changed."

"No strings attached. Honest," Marigold continued. "Just one friend giving comfort to another. Comfort sex."

"You mean pity sex."

"Absolutely not." Marigold was firm. Kasima didn't need her pity. A beautiful woman like her could get any lover she wanted. She thought it best to keep that last thought to herself. If that lover wasn't going to be her, she didn't want Kasima seeking one elsewhere either. "More like…friends with benefits. That's a thing, right?"

"Friends with benefits." Kasima's posture relaxed again as she chewed on a pretzel and, presumably, the idea.

"Just think of it as me comforting you, the same as you did for me with the beer cheese, which I declared better than sex, so if you think about it, you've already taken a riskier step by unleashing that level of comfort on me."

Kasima laughed. "That explanation is more convoluted than the premise of *Homestead Hollow*."

"I'm just saying the sex will probably be nothing compared to what you stirred up in me with the beer cheese."

Kasima's chestnut eyes smoldered. "We'll see about that."

* * *

Kasima wasn't exactly sure how to do this comfort sex thing, but there was one thing she knew—as divine as her beer cheese was, sex was definitely better. Especially if that sex was going to be with Marigold. Ever since that night at her condo, she had been aching to kiss her again. She just hadn't wanted to mess up their friendship. But if they had an agreement that this was just a friends-with-benefits situation—an arrangement that spelled out how things were going to go before feelings got messy—then what was the harm?

"I think I could get on board with this idea." She tentatively pulled Marigold to her and unzipped her hoodie, revealing the lacy pale-pink camisole she wore under it. Her pulse sped up, anticipating what else was in store for her. Comfort sex with Marigold sounded like a wonderful indulgence. As long as they both were aware of what they were doing, then everything would be fine. She kissed Marigold's neck, eliciting a moan in response. A delicious, needing, from-the-gut sound. The same sound she'd made after tasting the beer cheese for the first time. It seemed Marigold was into the indulgence of comfort sex as well. Kasima's heart pounded with excitement in her ears. It really had been too long since she'd had a good orgasm that wasn't at her own hand.

"Then it's agreed?" Marigold's question came out in a breathy register that only boosted her sex appeal. "We'll try the friends-with-benefits thing?"

What the hell. She was going for it.

"We'll try the friends-with-benefits thing."

Marigold's soft, warm hands slid down Kasima's back and slipped into the waistband of her yoga pants. She kicked out of her fuzzy slippers and continued nibbling Kasima's neck. "You're sure about this?"

"Mmmhmm."

"Wanna go to my room?" Her lusty words mashed against Kasima's skin.

"Mmmhmm."

Marigold slid her hands from Kasima's pants and turned her around to lead the way. Once in the bedroom, her hand slid into Kasima's hair, and she pulled her into another kiss. This time Kasima took her sweatshirt and camisole completely off, pushing her arms down to let them drop to the floor. Marigold's hands returned to Kasima's body, working under her T-shirt to unclasp her bra.

Despite it being a FWB situation, Kasima couldn't help but feel pleased by the lust reflected in Marigold's heavy-lidded eyes as she looked over her body. The desire plainly written on her face was a huge turn-on. Heat rushed downward to the apex between her legs. Before she realized how it had happened, they were in the bed, touching, kissing, and moving together. Kasima grabbed on to the back of Marigold's neck and buried her face in her hair, inhaling her fresh, green-tea scent. How had she never noticed how absolutely intoxicating it was before?

"I've got to hand it to you," Kasima murmured. "This was a brilliant idea."

"I think so." Marigold kissed her once on the lips before sliding down her body and off the edge of the bed, positioning herself between her legs.

Kasima ran her fingertips along her smooth skin, tracing every beautiful curve of her shoulders and enjoying the waves of pleasure Marigold gifted her with. She wanted to enjoy this swell of excitement and ride it as long as she could. She tried her best to focus on the smooth feel of the cotton sateen fabric of the sheets clutched in her fist and the cool breeze from the ceiling fan blowing over them, but the constant flicks of Marigold's tongue had other plans for her. With a yelp of surrender, she tumbled over the edge, and her orgasm swept her away to bliss.

"I'll say it again," she managed to say between gulps of air. "You are brilliant."

Marigold laughed throatily as she climbed back up to lie beside her. "You can say it as many times as you want."

Aftershocks ran through Kasima's body, little quakes of comfort.

"Cuddle me?" She grabbed at the sheets, tugging them up around them, wanting nothing more than to fall asleep in Marigold's capable arms. "Will you just hold me for a little while?"

"Of course."

They moved under the covers and Kasima curled against Marigold's warm body—her little spoon. They were a perfect fit. She sighed contentedly and sank into her very comforting embrace.

CHAPTER TWENTY-TWO

The next morning Marigold lay in bed waiting for her alarm to go off. The sheets still smelled like Kasima—all orange blossoms and sunshine, and they were still warm even though she'd rolled out of bed forty-five minutes earlier to run home and get ready for work at the brewery.

Images of the night they'd shared—one friend comforting another—flashed in her mind. They had drifted off to sleep after she'd given Kasima that first orgasm, but a couple of hours later she awoke to sensual neck kisses and a hand sneaking between her thighs. Round two was on, and it was just as steaming hot as the first. The feel of Kasima's legs wrapped around her waist, the taste of her salty skin just south of her collarbone, the perfect fit of their bodies spooning as they drifted off to slumber again. Marigold would've thought she'd be tossing and turning all night, unable to sleep after retrieving her wayward client from the police station, but after sharing a delicious meal and trading toe-curling orgasms, she'd been out for the count.

And waking up with Kasima still in her arms, that had been heavenly. The whole experience of being tangled up together in the sheets had been so much more than she'd anticipated. More sensual, more satisfying, more…binding than she'd expected. The pure joy that erupted in her chest even now as she inhaled the scent of Kasima's orange-blossom shampoo still present on the pillowcase was almost overwhelming.

It was then, with her face pressed to a pillow, desperate to hold on to the essence of the woman who had left her bed almost an hour earlier, that Marigold realized her mistake. She'd agreed to be friends with benefits with someone she had most definitely already fallen for.

* * *

When Marigold had checked her phone before leaving for work, there weren't any articles out yet detailing Ava's adventures the night before. But by the time she stepped into the McClancy-Jansen offices, she had a missed call and a text from Allison summoning her to her office. Some sort of story must have hit. Her stomach dropped. She was in no mood to receive an earful from her boss about how she was managing this client, but there was no sense in putting it off. If she didn't go to Allison, Allison would just track her down anyway and then she'd be caught on the defensive. After a quick stop in her own office to drop off her bags and give herself a quick look in the mirror, she reported in with her boss to get it over with.

"Have you seen this?" They had barely exchanged pleasantries before Allison got right to it, turning her monitor for Marigold's benefit.

She squinted to read the headline on the screen.

"Dakota Oakley Rides Again," Allison read out loud. A pause, probably for dramatic effect. "This is simply wonderful!"

Wonderful? The split image below the bold words showed Ava on the mechanical bull on one side and her being helped into the back of the squad car on the other. Yes, the young woman had taken two kinds of rides last night, and if Marigold hadn't arrived at the police station when she did, there may have even been a third. What the hell did Allison think was so great about that? It was all a complete mess.

"I'm sorry." Marigold shook her head. "You think a story about our underage client nearly starting a bar brawl, being kicked out of said bar, then being picked up by the police and taken to the station for a drunk and disorderly is 'simply wonderful'?"

"Are you kidding me? With the show gearing up for the season finale, this is exactly the kind of stunt that will ratchet up excitement for fans of *Homestead Hollow*. It's all so very Dakota Oakley. She was riding a mechanical bull for fuck's sake."

"And she was *arrested*." Marigold dragged out every syllable that last word to make sure her boss understood what had actually gone down. She couldn't believe Allison was just blowing right past that one crucial part of Ava's evening activities. She hadn't even asked about what had happened to their client after she was put in the cop car. She didn't ask if Ava was okay. All she seemed to care about was the success of the show. "They didn't end up actually charging her. She somehow managed to flirt her way out of it."

"Oh my God. Even better." Allison clapped her hands joyfully; her eyes were big with delight. They may as well have had dollar signs flashing in them like she was some kind of greedy cartoon character. "That is so Dakota Oakley."

"It was lucky is what it was. The Dakota Oakley shenanigans might be good for the show's ratings, but they're not good for Ava's career long term. *Homestead Hollow* isn't my client. Ava Ashford is. I have a duty to her that I intend to fulfill."

"And the better the show does, the better it is for Ava, don't you see? *Homestead Hollow* is about to really take off and when it does, Ava Ashford will be a household name. We don't want to lose her as a client just when everything seems to be going her way. So don't piss her off by clipping her wings. It's not your job to parent her."

Marigold's stomach tightened uncomfortably. Why had Allison said that thing about parenting her? Had Ava seen her sitting outside of her house watching to make sure she didn't leave again? Had she really been too strict with Ava about the whole drunken ordeal?

"That's not what I'm trying to do. I only wanted to..." She tried to run through everything that was said in the car, but it had been a long evening, and it felt like much longer than a mere twelve hours had passed. There was the scene at Tequila On Sunset, then the police station and dropping Ava off, and of course a full night of making love to Kasima. *Nope, don't go there now. Focus.* "Did Ava make a complaint about me? About something I said or did, I mean?"

"No, no. Nothing like that." Allison waved a hand in her direction and turned her attention back to her computer monitor. Marigold got the feeling she was being shooed away. "But we certainly don't want that. Our goal is to keep her happy. And to keep the publicity coming. That's all." Definitely dismissed.

Back in her own office, Marigold tried to focus on her work, but she couldn't push out of her mind the worry about how she was handling Ava. Her gut told her she should be tougher with the young actor—she was literally the voice of experience in this situation, since she'd been a teen star herself. Yet Allison was the boss and had the final say in how the agency managed their clients' careers. Defying her directives would only piss her off, and Allison had the ability to make her time at McClancy-Jansen very uncomfortable. Marigold had worked too hard and come too far with the agency to give up her current position there. One way or another, she was going to have to find a way to strike a balance with Allison's role as partner.

It made sense for her to phone and check in with Ava. Who wouldn't follow up with their client after an incident like the one the night before? But all of her calls went to Ava's voice mail, which did nothing to ease Marigold's concern that her client was displeased with her.

After a morning of poor focus and a feeling of burning dread in her belly, Marigold's afternoon trip to visit her mother actually seemed like a relief. A change of scenery could be what she needed to clear her head.

On the drive to the assisted living home, Marigold pondered the idea of asking Constance for advice on the Ava Ashford situation. People asked their parents for advice on things, that was a normal thing to do. Just because she'd never done it before as an adult herself didn't mean she couldn't ever.

Plus, Constance had always known how to manage Marigold's career. That time during a late-night shoot when Marigold and Elle had sneaked off set and went to a club though they were both underage, Constance had freaked the fuck out. She didn't say, "Simply wonderful!" or "That will ratchet up excitement!" She had grounded Marigold for three months.

Marigold could understand Constance's reaction better now, especially after Ava's shenanigans at Tequila On Sunset. When she had been on the teen drama *Sugar & Spice*, Marigold's character was a sweet and innocent type. Purity, or at least the appearance of it, was not only good for her role of Sugar, but it happened to be good for her career as a whole. Success in the role she had in hand would lead to more roles, thus even more success. With the gift of hindsight, she could see that there was a reason behind the strict rules Constance had insisted on imposing.

It wasn't Constance's management methods that Marigold had resented per se. It was her insistence that her daughter not date girls that had caused the fissure in their relationship. The pressure to constantly hide who she really was—to lie about it to others—was what had pushed Marigold to her limit. That was what caused their relationship to blow up the way it did.

But upon Marigold's arrival at the home, Constance barely looked up from her jigsaw puzzle to greet her, apparently not even recognizing that the woman who plopped down in the worn green leather armchair across the table from her was, in fact, her daughter. Forthcoming career advice was doubtful.

The irony of the situation wasn't lost on Marigold. She had never before considered asking Constance for advice on how to handle a client, and now that she could really use some input, it wasn't an option. Her stomach immediately squeezed with guilt. There were a lot of things she should have said to Constance when she had the chance. Like "thank you" or "I'm sorry." Would she ever get the opportunity to do that now? Deep down she knew what Constance would say regarding Ava anyway: Don't be so soft with the girl. Set her straight. But Constance had been her own boss. She didn't have an agency or an Allison to answer to. It wasn't exactly the same thing.

She studied Constance in her crocheted pink-hued shawl and fuzzy slippers, working so intently on completing the puzzle you would think her life depended on it. Maybe for her brain it did. At least she seemed content.

"How long have you been working on this one, Constance?" For a moment Marigold thought she wasn't going to even get a response, but then her mother looked up as if she was surprised to see her.

"Marigold, what are you doing here? Don't you have dance class today?"

"Not today. Actually, I haven't taken dance classes since I was a teenager. Remember, Constance? You used to come to every rehearsal and sit and crochet while waiting for me." Marigold was never sure if the verbal redirect would help. This time it seemed it did.

"Of course I remember." Constance sounded annoyed that the question was even asked. She paused her puzzling long enough to put her hands on her hips and stare her daughter down. There was the talent management Constance from the past. The look was somehow comforting to Marigold now. "I put in so many hours at that dance studio, I probably could've done that Shuffle off to Buffalo tap step right along with you."

"I bet you'd put me to shame. Tap was always my worst—"

Marigold stopped midsentence as something—or rather someone—leaving the residence caught her attention. She stood to get a better view through the large window on the far side of the room.

A slender woman with a large-brimmed hat and a navy-blue duster sweater that swirled around her ankles was rushing toward an idling car. Though her face was obscured by her get-up, there was something about her petite frame and the cocky way she glided across the drive that Marigold recognized. She could swear it was Ava.

But what the hell would Ava be doing at Juniper Hills? Had she finally sobered up and come after Marigold to tell her off for the lecture and surveillance the night before? But then, why would she be leaving? And just how would Ava know she would be at Juniper Hills anyway? Marigold had never even mentioned Constance or her condition, much less where she lived to Ava.

Marigold took a few steps toward the window, hoping to get a closer look, but it was too late. All she saw was the brown suede pointy-toed boot of the woman climbing into the back seat before the door closed and the car drove off. Definitely not the style Ava usually wore. It wasn't her. She just had her client on the brain, that was all. She shook her head to chase away the ridiculous thought and returned to her chair. Even if Ava was angry about their conversation the night before—even if she had complained to Allison—she wouldn't track Marigold down at Juniper Hills to tell her off. That would be outrageous, even for her. She would've just come to the office.

"What are you fussing around about, Marigold?" Constance looked at her like she just noticed she was visiting. Marigold was used to these reset moments. "Why don't you pull that chair closer and help me with this puzzle?"

Marigold's heart warmed as she scooted closer to the table as instructed and surveyed the loose pieces that still needed to find their spot in the picture. She needed to be present in the moment. Constance had never asked her for help with a puzzle before. She sure wasn't going to miss the opportunity to do so now. Worrying about work would have to wait. Constance was having a fairly good day, and she should enjoy it while they had it to share. They'd already lost too much time.

* * *

Kasima whistled "Hot to Go"—the last song she'd heard on the radio—as she walked the brewery floor. The fermentation of the first full batch of Hooray For Howlywood—all four hundred sixty-five gallons' worth—was almost complete. Canning would occur in the next few days, and it would be ready to go in plenty of time for the live launch party.

It was hard to believe that the event was only two weeks away. In her heart she already knew this was going to be their biggest and best fundraiser for SoCal Wildlife Rescue yet, and that filled her with pride. It also filled her chest with a gratitude that felt like beams of sunshine for Marigold and all of the help she'd provided in this endeavor.

Marigold. Remembering waking up wrapped safely in her arms after the coziest slumber she'd experienced in a long time gave Kasima another warm and sunny feeling. Warm and sunny, and just a little bit dirty, but in a very good way. Marigold had been right—that night of comfort had been exactly what she needed. And why not move forward with their friends-with-benefits arrangement? They were consenting adults—they could pursue this kind of thing if they wanted to. Kasima had awakened that morning feeling content and cared for and totally refreshed. And from that point on, she had sailed through her day. Like she was walking on sunshine. *That's a good song too*, she thought and as the tune in her head switched, she did a little skip step, shoulder shake combination that didn't go unnoticed by Spencer as he came through the back door of the brewery.

"Someone's in a good mood," he teased. "What's gotten into you?"

If he only knew.

"Can't a girl just have a good day?"

"Of course a girl can." He gave her shoulder a gentle squeeze. "I'm just happy to see it. A good mood looks good on you. Since you've been with Marigold you've been wearing happiness well. I think it's great."

Was it that obvious that she'd slept with Marigold? Her chest tightened and that cloud she'd been floating along on all day deflated a little as she made sense of what her brother actually meant by "been with Marigold." Not necessarily "been with" her having sex, but more like "been with" her as girlfriends. Because even though she'd had the best intentions about coming clean, she still hadn't admitted to her family that she and Marigold were not truly a couple.

And how could she with the way Spencer was grinning at her? There was relief written all over his face. Relief that his little sister was finally showing signs that she was going to be okay. That things might be normal again. "Um, thanks."

Spencer gave her a playful punch in the arm before continuing on his way to do whatever task had brought him into the brewery building in the first place.

She was going to have to face her family's disappointment and their potential worry about her lying problem when she came clean with them eventually, but with the release event coming up so soon, perhaps it would be best to announce the fake breakup afterwards. It would be too awkward for everyone otherwise, and she needed the release party to be as successful as possible. She didn't like being untruthful with her family, but for now it seemed like the easiest way forward for everyone. It was only for a couple more weeks. Everything would be fine until then.

CHAPTER TWENTY-THREE

"I can't believe we're only one week out from the release party. Is your family excited?" Marigold took a sip from her can of Hooray For Howlywood. Kasima had surprised her by serving it that night. She'd thought she'd have to wait until the big event to get her hands on the limited-edition brew. Kasima had pointed out that they needed something special to commemorate their television viewing that evening, and she was absolutely right—the West Coast IPA was delicious and perfect for the occasion.

"I can't believe it's the season finale," Kasima countered as she grabbed a handful of popcorn. It was the same snack they'd shared the very first time they'd watched the show together, only this time they were at Kasima's apartment for the viewing. "Do you know how it's going to end? Do you have some kind of insider info from working with Ava? No, wait. Don't tell me if you do. I don't want any spoilers."

Marigold laughed. It wasn't that long ago that Kasima hadn't even heard of Dakota Oakley and *Homestead Hollow*, and now, it seemed, she was a fan. It was a very cute look on her. "I'm not going to spoil anything, but I do have some good news for you—the show has been picked up for a second and a third season."

"They're just finishing season one and they've already committed to two more?" she asked around a mouthful of popcorn. "That's incredible. I bet Ava's excited."

"I think her exact response was 'Lez ride!'" Marigold clocked Kasima's befuddled expression and realized she might need clarification. "She's really working to make that phrase stick. I just hope she celebrates responsibly. I don't want to jinx anything, but she's been quiet lately. I can't help but feel like she's overdue for another bout of shenanigans. I hope I'm wrong, of course, but…"

"From your lips to God's ears," Kasima said before reaching over and giving Marigold's thigh an enthusiastic squeeze. "Shhhh! It's starting. Here we go."

The warmth of Kasima's hand on her leg caused a jolt of pleasure to shoot up to the V between Marigold's legs. She hoped that the redness she was certain was creeping into her cheeks would be read as excitement for the episode and not lust for her friend. Friends with benefits were definitely not supposed to have the emotional tug she felt to Kasima. She took another long drink and hoped the cold beer would help her chill out. She was only there to watch a show with a friend. Nothing more. They were just friends.

* * *

"There were survivors on the other side of the country?" Kasima couldn't remember the last time she felt so invested in a television program. She'd always been more of a go-out-and-do gal than a sit-in-and-watch one. But this show was so sensational, so damn over the top, she was hooked. And the cliffhanger ending, where a ragtag bunch of East Coast apocalypse survivors found their way into the outer limits of the town of Homestead Hollow had her wanting more. No wonder the network had extended the contract. "I did not see that coming."

"I've gotta admit, I didn't either. How long do you think it will be before the werewolves—"

Kasima's phone dinged with an incoming text. "Oh, it's my mom." She scanned the message. "Oh geez."

Marigold's eyebrows scrunched together in concern. "Everything okay?"

"Yes." She tapped out a quick response and tossed the phone back onto the coffee table. "She thinks it's just a matter of time before Dakota gets tangled up with that tall blonde that's traveling with the East Coasters."

"No! She just finally got together with Charlotte," Marigold protested, but then the entirety of Kasma's words seemed to register. "Wait. Your mom is watching *Homestead Hollow* too?"

"Yep." Kasima grinned. "Once she found out that you're Ava Ashford's manager, she wanted to check out her work. She ended up enjoying the show so much that she kept on watching. Now she's hooked too."

"Constance would never watch *Homestead Hollow*," Marigold mused.

"Constance is your mom, right?" Kasima tried to remember if Marigold had ever mentioned anything about her mother before but came up blank. They'd talked a lot about Kasima's family, but Marigold had never really shared anything about her own. "Does she follow any of the things your clients do?"

* * *

Marigold sucked in a breath. She hadn't meant to open the door to a conversation about Constance, but here she was. "I don't think she's paid my career any attention in years." It was a flippant statement. Not entirely untrue, but Kasima deserved better than that. She sighed.

"It's…complicated."

"Complicated?" Kasima's confused expression melted into concern. "Do you want to talk about it?"

Talk about it? Marigold never talked about it. To anyone. Elle knew, but she had known Constance since their child acting days. Marigold's day-to-day routine at her job centered around keeping the less shiny parts of people's lives quiet. She liked to keep the less shiny parts of her own life quiet too. And she certainly never talked about Constance with any of women she had casually dated—there was never any reason to bring up her sad feelings with someone she wasn't going to be in a long-term romantic relationship with.

That wasn't exactly the case with her and Kasima, of course. They weren't going to be in a long-term romantic relationship because they were just friends. Or maybe friends with benefits, although she wasn't sure she could keep that up either without becoming too attached in ways Kasima had made it clear she didn't want.

God, everything is so complicated now that we've slept together. It wasn't just the feelings for Kasima that were blooming in her that she wasn't supposed to be having that were bringing on this heavy feeling. Suddenly she was feeling the full weight of the sadness and guilt she'd been carrying around since her teens. The stifling tightness in her chest that sometimes came late at night when she thought about everything her mother had done for her and her career and all the years that they had lost.

Kasima was sitting there, not expecting anything from her, just studying her with kind eyes and willing to help if she could. It might feel good to unload to someone she could trust, and no matter what label they put on their relationship, Kasima was definitely someone she could trust.

She took a deep breath and began. "Three years ago, Constance fell in her home and suffered a traumatic brain injury. As a result, she gets confused, can't remember things, ends up really frustrated—even angry sometimes. Occasionally she even forgets who I am or she talks to me like I'm still a kid. Often times I end up really frustrated too, which just opens up a whole other level of guilt for me." She held up a hand at Kasima's apologetic look. "You didn't know. It's okay. I never talk about it. At the time she fell, she lived in Missouri with her husband, my stepfather. But I didn't find out about any of this until a year after her accident, when her husband passed away suddenly and the assisted living home she was in called me. Even though we hadn't talked in over a decade, she still had me listed as her next of kin."

"Marigold, that's terrible." Kasima grasped her hand on the couch cushions between them. "I'm so sorry to hear about your mother. It must be so hard—for the both of you. But you went for over a decade without speaking? What happened?"

Marigold pressed her eyes shut, willing the tears not to fall. An ugly feeling that she hadn't ever spoken aloud knocked around in her belly. It was one she'd been chained to, dragging along with her these past two years. One she'd been trying to ignore by burying herself in her work. But now with her guard down, with Kasima holding on to her and keeping her safe, it seemed like saying it to someone else might just be the release she needed.

She took a shaky breath. "I feel so guilty that we lost all those years where we could have mended our relationship, and I know it's my fault. I was the one who caused the rift between us in the first place." Despite her valiant efforts, tears slid down her cheeks. "I was sixteen and wrapping up my second season on *Sugar & Spice*. One afternoon, I was in my trailer making out with a girl who was an extra on the show that particular week, and Constance walked in on us. She totally lost it. She started yelling at me about showing some class and decorum and she chased poor Jenni-what's-her-name right out of the trailer. Then she blessed me with yet another of her lectures on maintaining a 'certain image' both on and off camera."

"Oh, Marigold." Kasima's eyes were full of pity, probably sensing the direction the story was going to take.

"Yeah, and it didn't help anything when I told her that kissing Jenni wasn't just a whim. I liked girls, not boys, and I wasn't going to pretend to be someone I wasn't anymore. I wasn't going to lie about who I was. Constance had responded by saying, 'Your entire career is built on you playing the part of the girl next door, an America's sweetheart type. You can't be a *lesbian*.'"

Kasima shook her head. "You must've been crushed."

Even thinking back on the moment all these years later felt like a punch to the belly to Marigold. "I was, but I was pissed off too. And being a teenager who thought she was a big freaking deal, I reacted impulsively. I mean, why on earth couldn't I be both the All-American girl next door and a lesbian? The only conclusion

I could draw from Constance's reaction was that she wanted to control all aspects of my life, and she was using her status as my manager to do just that."

Kasima shifted beside her on the couch and put a comforting hand on Marigold's knee. "So, you told her that's what you thought."

"That's not all," Marigold started, but then she paused and chewed on the inside of her cheek. She wasn't that impulsive, angry teenager anymore, yet she still felt embarrassed to admit she had behaved in that manner. But Kasima was her friend; she could be honest with her. "You know, up until that point, I'd begrudgingly gone along with many of Constance's rules and policies for my career. I'd avoided activities that could potentially end in injury or even bruising, I'd kept up a strict skincare regimen, and adhered to a diet and workout routine designed to keep me thinner than was natural for my body build. I'd sacrificed a lot in the name of Constance's vision for my acting career. But denying me the rush I'd experienced when I let Jenni the extra slip her hand under my shirt during that kiss—that was a bridge too far."

All these years later Marigold could still remember the dizzying roar of anger in her ears when she faced off with Constance that day. "Headstrong and hurt, I looked her dead in the eye and said, 'Who I want to be with is my choice. I'm sick of you calling the shots. It's like you're living through me and it's pathetic. You're no longer my manager. You're fired.'" She paused when Kasima gasped. "Yeah, it was a long frosty week in our house before I declared I was filing for emancipation and Constance did me one better and kicked me out right then. Constance didn't have other clients, she was my manager out of necessity. When I shut her out of my life, she effectively lost her daughter and her job. Shortly after that she moved away from California and the divide between us stretched even further with each year that passed. Each of us too stubborn to try to breach it and make things right. Until it was too late."

Kasima said nothing while Marigold got it all out. She just listened supportively, held her hand, and occasionally brushed a tear away.

"You don't know Constance, but back when I was a kid, she was a force. And she was a hell of a manager. I can see that now," Marigold admitted with a bitter laugh. "That's one thing that working with Ava has shown me. Constance only pushed me to make my image a priority over my personal choices because she was my manager and it was the smart thing to do in the moment for my career. I know it wasn't her intention for me to never come out. She simply wanted me not to do it while playing that particular role on *Sugar & Spice*." She laughed again. "The show was canceled the year after Constance moved to Missouri anyway, and I could've dated whomever the hell I wanted. Instead, I threw a fit and dug my heels in and pushed away the one person who loved me. I lived with Elle and her mother for a while, but after the show ended that final season, I'd had it with the whole acting thing. It just felt like more pretending to me. I quit the business and went to college."

"I'm so sorry, Marigold. It sounds like this has really been weighing you down." Kasima passed her a handful of tissues. "I'm sure Constance has some regret about her part in what happened as well. And I'm sure she's glad to have you back in her life now. Do you think maybe she's forgiven you, and now you need to show yourself some grace and forgive yourself?"

Marigold shook her head. She didn't deserve that grace. "I think this is just my cross to bear for the way I treated her back then, not to mention all those years after."

"Could you try talking to her about it?"

"I hate to spend the time when she's lucid bringing up bad feelings. I don't want to upset her, you know? I want to make things as easy for her as I can now." She mopped a hand across her face. "If that means swallowing my own bad feelings, so be it. I owe her that much at least."

"That's understandable," Kasima said, pulling her closer and rubbing a gentle hand down Marigold's back. "You want to do what's best for your mother. It's just that as someone looking at the situation from the outside, I can't help worrying about you too." She planted a sweet kiss on the top of her head.

The tension drained from her shoulders—not completely, but more than it had in days—and Marigold sank into Kasima's side. The comfort of unburdening herself, by saying it all to someone else, left a space in her for peace to roll in like a thick fog—blanketing everything within her, holding it still and quiet. Pressed up against Kasima was a wonderful place to be. Suddenly she was very aware of Kasima's orange-blossom scent, the same one that had lingered on the pillowcase after they'd spent the night together. Her heart thumped, breaking up that haze of peace as she recalled the longing she'd felt when Kasima left her bed that sweet morning.

This was a dangerous line of thought. She was vulnerable and already much more attached to Kasima than she should be. She appreciated the comfort Kasima provided, but she couldn't do the friends-with-benefits thing. Not that night. Maybe not ever again. It would be a lie, first of all. And she was only going to end up hurt. Her feelings were growing too strong, and if she admitted that to Kasima, she risked chasing her away all together and ruining their friendship. No. Best just to call it a night before the question of staying over arose.

"Sorry I've been blabbering on. It's late, and I have an early morning tomorrow. I should probably get going."

As Marigold pushed up from the couch, she registered the bewilderment on Kasima's face, but she didn't let it deter her from making her hasty exit. She simply said goodbye and left before either of them got hurt.

* * *

How did so much popcorn end up on the couch instead of in our mouths?

Kasima plucked a few more kernels from between the cushions and deposited them back into the bowl before gathering the empty beer cans and taking it all to the kitchen. She put the whole mess in the sink to be dealt with in the morning. After the excitement of the TV show's finale, her mood had totally tanked when Marigold had suddenly rushed out. Maybe she'd felt awkward after sharing everything about her mother. It was a really heavy and sad story, and Kasima had felt honored that she'd trusted her enough to tell it to her. She'd thought they were really connecting. Deepening their friendship.

On top of that, she'd kind of expected that they would be spending the night together again. She was looking forward to more of their friends-with-benefits arrangement. She hadn't been able to get the memory of their steamy night together out of her mind, and she'd been hoping for a repeat performance.

Dejectedly, she climbed the stairs to her bedroom and changed into her PJs. She really shouldn't be so bummed out. Marigold was certainly under no obligation to stay over. Maybe she wasn't into the sex as much as Kasima was. That was fair. Assuming they were going to end up sleeping together every time they hung out made them seem like a couple, and they definitely weren't a couple. That was the whole point of the friends-with-benefits arrangement in the first place.

Kasima slid between the cool sheets of her bed and stretched her limbs, taking up as much space as she could. She was fine alone. Marigold didn't consider them a couple, and that was why she didn't feel obligated to stay. They were just friends. And that was exactly what Kasima wanted.

Wasn't it?

CHAPTER TWENTY-FOUR

"I've got to hand it to you, Sunday Funday was a brilliant idea." Marigold took another sip of her margarita and adjusted her wide-brimmed hat.

Kasima had invited her over for an afternoon of carefree—and, most importantly, work-free—lounging on her rooftop paradise, and although Marigold had insisted on having her phone close by in case of client emergency, she'd arrived armed with sunblock and a romance novel, ready for a day of relaxation.

"After all the extra hours we've put in working on the special release, we deserve it. The only thing we have to think about is what we want to order for dinner." Kasima was a total California girl in palm tree-print board shorts and a bikini top. Not just anyone could pull off that neon pink color, but with her ash-brown hair and tanned skin, it worked. The overall effect was a thing of beauty.

Comparatively, Marigold had elected to cover up a good deal of her ivory skin with a lightweight floral print boho cover-up over her modest one-piece swimsuit and, of course, her trusty straw hat. But still, she couldn't deny there was something restorative about spending time in the sunshine.

"I swear, I'm not even thinking about Ava Ashford today," she said, reaching for a handful of grapes from the fruit tray Kasima had set out for them to snack on.

"And I am hardly thinking about the midsummer beers I still have to theme and name."

"I can't help but notice that 'hardly thinking' is actually thinking," Marigold said, shooting her a wry look. "You're not supposed to be thinking about brewing beer at all."

"In fairness, I'm not thinking about the beer I'm currently brewing." Kasima sat up to refill their margaritas. "It's more like I'm casually pondering future beers."

"Oh, yes. That wrinkle in your brow totally says, 'casually pondering.' Seriously. Total elevens up there."

"I can't help it." Kasima sighed as she settled back on her side of the horseshoe-shaped teak sofa. "Beer is just part of who I am. It's in my blood."

Marigold took another gulp of her margarita. "I think the beer in your blood is going to be in competition with tequila by the time we kill this pitcher."

"Good point. But there's nothing like the kick of lime on a hot summer day." Her eyebrows popped up excitedly above the round rims of her sunglasses. "Oh! I should work a hint of lime into my hazy IPA."

"Okay, we're doing this," Marigold quipped, but she really didn't mind talking beer with Kasima. She only needed the escape from her own work. "You've got a lime-inspired hazy IPA, which I agree is very summer forward. What else?"

"Probably another IPA and either a porter or a stout to mix it up a bit. But it's not the beers themselves that I'm stumped on. It's the theme and names for the trio."

"Something that combines summer and Hollywood," Marigold mused. "Does the theme always need to be old school Hollywood?"

"My dad has always preferred to stick with the classics. Things that have stood the test of time and that people will connect with Hollywood. Why?"

"I'm thinking something from the eighties might be fun," Marigold suggested. "That's like, forty years ago—I'd label that vintage at this point."

Kasima removed her sunglasses and squinted at her. "What did you have in mind for names? Puns of movie names? Something like Raiders Of The Lost Hops or Dead Porter Society?"

Marigold chewed on her bottom lip and considered that for a moment before clarifying, "When I think of those eighties classics, what really sticks with me is the music. Movies from that era had the best soundtracks. I mean, think about it—*Top Gun*, *Footloose*, *Dirty Dancing*—all full of songs people know. We could work with some titles and come up with puns for beer names."

Kasima nodded as if the idea was taking hold with her. "Okay… any specific ideas?"

"This is just off the top of my head, but you could brew a beer with high ABV and call it 'Danger Zone.' You know, like the Kenny Loggins's song from *Top Gun*."

"An alcohol content high enough to be associated with danger? That sounds a little off-putting." Kasima frowned. "What else have you got?"

"Hey, there are no bad ideas in a brainstorming session." Marigold paused to stick her tongue out at Kasima before trying again. "They use 'It Had to Be You' in *When Harry Met Sally*. How about It Had To Be Brew? Wait! Or maybe Don't Brew Forget About Me, like that song from *The Breakfast Club*!"

Kasima's joyful burst of laughter was not only contagious, it released a flurry of butterflies in Marigold's belly. "Don't Brew Forget About Me is a horrendous name for a beer. But you've certainly given me something to think about." When their giggles subsided, she continued, "Let's put a pin in this for the moment. We agreed, no work, no worries today, and I'm ready to hold up my end of the bargain, starting by making a fresh pitcher of margaritas." She divided the remaining liquid in the pitcher between their glasses before standing. "Can I get you anything else?"

Marigold welcomed the cold drink as a way to combat the heat in her cheeks that remained from the pleasure of making Kasima laugh, but she suspected the alcohol could catch up to them soon if they didn't eat something substantial. "Sounds perfect. I'll start looking at some dinner options before we end up in the danger zone ourselves."

Her gaze stayed on Kasima's slender yet muscular back as she slipped back into the house. She could abide by the no-work portion of their agreement, but she was finding it damn hard not to worry. How the hell was she going to continue to keep those more-than-friends feelings she was developing for Kasima under wraps?

* * *

Kasima, with one hand holding a full pitcher and the other holding her phone, used her hip to push through the door as she returned to the rooftop oasis. She'd picked up the call from her dad while she was making the margaritas, but now she was anxious to get back to her time with Marigold. They'd been having a lovely afternoon, and she found herself compelled to give Marigold her full attention while they had this downtime together. Purely because she enjoyed her company, and surely not just because her pulse sped up every time she caught a glimpse of Marigold's cleavage peeking out of her gauzy sarong.

She set the pitcher on the teak table and said into the phone, "No, Dad. I'm sure. We're just going to order in tonight. But thanks for the invite."

Marigold was refilling their drinks and giving her a questioning look as Kasima set down her phone and returned to her spot on the chaise. "There was an invite?"

"Oh, yeah. My parents are having Spence's family over and wanted to see if we wanted to join them." She realized the implication as soon as she'd said it—her parents were inviting their kids and their kids' people to dinner. Spence had Olivia and Matty; Kasima had Marigold. At least that was what her parents believed. Her mouth was suddenly dry, and she could only hope that Marigold had missed the insinuation.

"It's so nice of your family to invite me to dinner, especially since they think we broke up. I mean, I know in traditional lesbian culture friends with exes is the norm, but…wait." Her brow furrowed and the corners of her mouth turned down. "You told them we aren't together, right?"

"Of course." The lie slipped out before she could consider it, but she just couldn't stand that look of disappointment on Marigold's face. It didn't matter anyway. She would straighten the whole thing out with her parents in less than a week—as soon as the launch party was behind them. This was barely a lie. It was more like borrowing time.

"Good." Marigold looked so relieved, Kasima's ears burned with shame. She shook her head. "I'm sure it seems ridiculous, but you know being my authentic self is just so important to me and—"

"No," Kasima interrupted. Suddenly the tequila in her stomach sloshed uncomfortably. She knew how Marigold felt, and yet she'd continued to perpetuate the lie to her parents. And just as bad, she realized, she'd been lying to Marigold the whole time too. "It's not ridiculous. It's important to you, and that's perfectly understandable." *And anyone who really cared about you would respect that*, she berated herself. She would make this right, just as soon as the party was over.

"Kasima?" Marigold waved her hand in front of her face as if trying to pull her back from her far away thoughts. "You okay? I topped off your margarita. Drink up."

She did as she was told and hoped the cool drink would ease the thickness in her throat. As soon as the party was over. The very next day. She would tell her parents the truth and make it all right.

CHAPTER TWENTY-FIVE

The taproom was never empty at lunchtime on Thursdays, but today they were closed for business. It was finally the day Kasima had been working toward—the Hooray For Howlywood release party. Enchanted Hops Taproom had closed the night before and wouldn't reopen until the guests were set to arrive.

She had personally wiped down every table and chair in the place that morning, and after lunch she'd enlisted Spencer's help to hang decorations. Now with just about everything in place for the evening she was feeling pleased with herself for a job well done. Pleased with herself and with Marigold because as she surveyed the room—from the line of beer cans on the bar with the brightly colored labels the two of them had designed to the posters on the walls Marigold had printed up bearing those same images and even the balloon bouquets in those same vivid hues that had arrived only moments earlier—all around her were signs that Marigold had had a major hand in making this event happen.

A glance at her watch told her she still had half an hour before she would need to go home and get dolled up for the party. Just enough time to cross a few bar tasks off her list. She slid behind the bar to check the ice levels in the bins and then made sure the glassware was completely stocked. As she headed to the dish room to collect any additional glasses that could be returned to the bar, her mind wandered back to Marigold. Would the two of them still hang out after the party was over and they didn't have the excuse of event planning to bring them together? Kasima hoped so. She had a lot of fun with Marigold, and she didn't want to lose that. Even though their friends-with-benefits arrangement had fizzled out just as quickly as it had begun, she still wanted to maintain the friendship part.

If she had her druthers, she wouldn't mind revisiting the benefits portion too. That night they'd spent together had been incredible—a night of pleasure indelibly inked in her memory. She still got goose bumps on her arms just thinking about it. But she hadn't wanted to push the issue with Marigold. She didn't want her to think sex was the only thing she liked about her. There were so many things about Marigold that she admired, like her strong business acumen and the way she really cared about her clients—heaven knew she'd witnessed her going above and beyond for Ava Ashford time and time again. Marigold was a fun, intelligent, creative person, and Kasima was drawn to all of it. It had been a bonus to discover the sexual chemistry between them as well, but it wasn't necessary to act on it for her to want to remain in Marigold's orbit. Although she still did want to act on it.

When Kasima returned to the taproom with an armful of server trays she'd pulled off of the dish room drying rack, her father was standing in the center of the space, smiling and slowly spinning as if taking it all in.

"Kas, you and Marigold have outdone yourselves. This is going to be one hell of a party."

"I think we're going to do SoCal Wildlife Rescue proud with the sales of this one," she agreed and stepped into his embrace.

"Well, you've already made your old man proud." He kissed the top of her head.

As happy as she'd felt only seconds before, she couldn't ignore the burning kernel of guilt in her gut. All her parents had ever done was provide her with unconditional love and support, and here she was still lying to them about being in a relationship with Marigold. She swallowed hard against the lump rising in her throat and reminded herself it was literally only for one more day. After the party she could tell them she and Marigold broke up—that they decided they were better off as friends or something like that. One more little white lie and that would be that. She could go back to her normal, nonlying life. "Thanks, Dad."

It was only for one more day.

* * *

Thursday night the release party was in full swing when Marigold saw an open spot at the packed bar and squeezed in, signaling to the bartender for a Hooray For Howlywood. She'd been holding back on consumption—wanting to keep a clear head as the evening began, but now she was ready to relax and enjoy it. Based on crowd size alone, the event was clearly a success. People had turned out in droves to get a taste of Kasima's special creation, and they seemed to be sticking around and enjoying the party vibe in the taproom.

Then there was the wonder that was Kasima herself. Usually so content to remain behind the scenes, tonight she was shining like the brightest lights in Hollywood. A long way from the nervous brewmaster who first sat down to record that bumbling podcast, she was now a true star as she worked the room, the passion for her product plain on her beautiful face as she talked about the Enchanted Hops Brewing Company, Hooray For Howlywood, and their fundraising efforts for SoCal Wildlife Rescue. She personified the event's success.

Marigold hitched her hip onto the barstool and took a sip of beer. Those painted-on jeans Kasima was wearing paired with her black Enchanted Hops tank top were a sight to behold. Seeing Kasima's bare, tanned shoulders took Marigold right back to that night they spent together—when they were wrapped in her sheets. She sucked in a deep breath, ready to admonish herself for going down that path—longing for something more with

Kasima—when the truth hit her. She couldn't keep existing in this in-between, holding in her emotions. She didn't want to.

She had to be honest with Kasima about her feelings. In the beginning she'd believed she could keep up the just friends act, but the more time they'd spent together, the clearer it had become to her—she was falling in love with Kasima. It wasn't fair to either of them for her to pretend otherwise. She would tell her. Not tonight, while Kasima was having her moment of glory, but tomorrow or the next day. She would shoot her shot and tell Kasima how she really felt.

Just then, Kasima caught her eye and flashed her that heart-stopping, confident smile. That was all it took to cement the idea in Marigold's mind. All the chaos of the party around them dropped away and time seemed to slow down. As Kasima approached, her ash-brown hair shimmered and swung around her like she was moving in slow motion. The light from the livestream camera backlit her, giving her an aura—a glow like an angel. Marigold's breath caught—she wasn't falling in love with Kasima. She was already there.

"How are you holding up, superstar?" Marigold asked when Kasima was finally close enough to hear her. "Looks like the brew is a huge hit. Congratulations."

Kasima reached out and squeezed her upper arm. "None of this would be possible without you. I mean, look at this turnout. You made that happen."

"I guess we make a pretty good team." Warmth spread through Marigold as she returned a proud smile. Together they had accomplished something truly awesome.

"You know, I'm starting to think we really do." Kasima bit her bottom lip and those golden flecks sparkled in her eyes. Was it possible she was feeling the same way about the two of them? That they were ready to take a step toward being more than friends?

Maybe she shouldn't wait to tell Kasima how she felt about her. Maybe now was the perfect time. The happy hum in her core sure didn't want her to wait any longer.

"Kasima, I…" She hadn't thought through exactly what she would say. What perfect words would win the day. "I wanted to—"

"Hey, everybody!" Brian's voice boomed from the center of the room. "Can I have your attention for just a moment?"

"We agreed Dad should be the one to make the closing remarks," Kasima said as the crowd hushed and turned their attention to Brian. Marigold nodded and swallowed hard. She didn't want to lose her nerve, but at least the break in their conversation gave her a chance to decide how to best say all the things she needed to express. Like everyone else, she turned her gaze to Brian.

"My family and I, as well as the entire staff of Enchanted Hops Brewing Company, would like to say a heartfelt thank you to all of you for coming out tonight to support SoCal Wildlife Rescue. I want to say a special thank you to my daughter, Kasima, who created the delicious brew that you've been enjoying all evening." He paused while the crowd applauded.

Beside her Kasima beamed and blew a kiss to her dad. Marigold absolutely adored the way the Powell family interacted with one another. So loving, so supportive of one another. And the way they had accepted her into the fold from minute one made her heart sing. She hadn't realized how much she'd missed being part of a family until they'd kind of taken her in. Or, more like, swept her up in their current. She almost laughed out loud at the thought. That was honestly more what it had been like. Regardless, she was grateful for it.

Brian raised his arms to quiet the crowd again. "And I would be totally remiss if I didn't thank the woman who made this party tonight happen, my daughter's girlfriend, Marigold Luxe."

Applause broke out again, but instead of the elation that normally came with recognition for a job well done, Marigold's stomach dropped. Her head swiveled sharply toward Kasima.

"Did your dad just refer to me as your 'girlfriend'? Why? Why would he say that?"

Any thought that perhaps Brian had just misspoken dissipated as Kasima turned to face her. The sparkle that had previously filled those nut-brown eyes had been replaced by guilt. Marigold's whole body tensed up as Kasima stammered an explanation.

"My family still thinks we're a couple," she confessed. "I swear I was going to tell them the truth, I just somehow didn't get around to it, and I figured with the special release and the party happening, it was just best to—"

"Stop." Marigold put her hands over her ears, partly because she didn't what to hear any of the excuses coming out of Kasima's mouth and partly to try to halt the pounding in her ears. "You're telling me that all this time your family has believed we were actually girlfriends, yet you've been holding me at arm's length because you didn't want to date anyone to guard your heart from getting broken again? I guess you don't have the same concern for other people's hearts."

Marigold hadn't meant to say that last part out loud—to admit that her heart hadn't been as well protected, but while she was speaking, the wave of anger that had originally washed over her had receded slightly, making way for hurt and embarrassment to seep in.

Kasima winced as if she'd been slapped. "You didn't exactly—"

"Don't." Marigold's voice rose the more she spoke. She knew people were looking at them, but she didn't care. "All this time we've been hanging out together and working together you've been lying to your family and to me. It's like you've just been using me."

Kasima's eyes went round, but before she had the chance to respond, Brian stepped between the two of them. "Girls, what is going on? Is everything okay?"

"No. We're not okay." Marigold spoke before Kasima could find her voice. This man—and his whole family—had been so kind to her and meanwhile she'd effectively been lying to him about who she really was. Not intentionally, but lying nonetheless. She wouldn't do it any longer. "We just broke up."

She gave Kasima one last hard glare, refusing to be swayed by the tears she saw in her eyes. Kasima had dug this hole herself. She could figure out how to climb out of it. Without another word, Marigold turned on her heel and walked out.

CHAPTER TWENTY-SIX

"Tell me again. Why is it a bad thing that the woman you wish was your girlfriend is telling people she's your girlfriend?" Elle was following as Marigold moved through her living room with a feather duster Friday morning.

"It's not about saying the word or not saying the word." Marigold tried again to explain. "I feel like such a fool. Spending time with Kasima's family—working with them—and all along they thought I was dating their daughter. They were so kind to me, and I was basically nonstop lying to their faces. You know I hate having to hide who I really am."

She reached the wand up to the top of the bookshelves which, based on the dust particles that were dispersed in its wake, had been neglected for too long.

"Oh my God. We need to get you a good cleaning service." Elle paused to sneeze. "Would you please knock off the angry cleaning for five minutes and talk to me?"

"I don't have anything else to say on the subject." But she flung the duster toward the sliding glass door. She'd take it outside and give it a good shake later. "Kasima lied to her family, and she lied to me. And in the process made me into a liar too. It's all a total fucking mess. I'm just horrified that the Powells think I'm a big ol' liar."

Elle's blank stare at this pronouncement was less than satisfying, so Marigold grabbed a throw pillow from the sofa and gave it a good fluffing.

"So, you're mad because you think your reputation with Kasima's family has been marred by this." Elle appeared to mull that over as she joined Marigold in fluffing the remainder of the pillows. "Do you think that's really at the crux of your feelings here? I mean, you don't know what those folks are thinking. And why does that matter so much to you anyway? You've told more than a few untruths about your clients over the years. What's the difference?"

Marigold tossed the pillow she'd been holding at Elle. "First of all, that's not telling untruths, that's spin. And secondly, I don't want that family to think that about me in case me and..." She shook her head and plopped down on the sofa. "I just don't want to be known as a liar, okay?"

Elle gently sat beside her. Her voice was softer when she spoke again. "You don't want them to think badly of you in case you and Kasima really do start dating. Is that what you were going to say?"

Yep, she nailed it.

"It doesn't matter." She blew out a long, surrendering breath. "No matter what she's been telling her family, Kasima doesn't want to be in a relationship—with me or anyone else. She's been completely transparent about that from the start. I'm the idiot who didn't listen to her and went and fell for her regardless of that. It just really felt like we had a connection." She paused to sniff back the threatening tears. "I was actually going to tell Kasima last night how I felt about her. Like I said, I feel so foolish."

"Hmmm." Elle wrinkled her nose.

"What?"

"It's just that you weren't exactly being honest with Kasima about things up to that point either." Elle had that look on her face that she got when she was dealing with her teenage daughter's antics. Marigold had seen it on more than one occasion. "Maybe you're not totally blameless in this situation, Mari."

Marigold's ribs tightened. That wasn't right at all. Sure, she hadn't told Kasima she was falling in love with her, but that was only because she was trying to respect their agreement. She was about to say as much when her phone rang again. *Saved by the bell.* "I better get that."

She swiped past the notification of three missed calls and picked up Allison's current one.

"Why the hell are you ignoring my calls?" Allison wasted no time with pleasantries. "Ava Ashford is here to see you. Did you forget about a meeting?"

"A meeting?" Marigold was certain she had no meeting with Ava on her schedule. Her day had been clear. It was the only reason she'd felt comfortable even taking a personal day. "No. There was nothing on my calendar today."

"Well, she's here and she wants to speak to you, so get your ass into the office."

"Allison, I told you I was taking a personal day." She stood her ground. "I'm not coming into the office."

"And *I* told *you* that we're going to do whatever it takes to keep this client," Allison snapped. "That means jumping when she says, 'jump.' Get here." She clicked off the call before Marigold could argue further.

"Let me guess," Elle said as she studied Marigold. "Another Ava Ashford emergency."

"At least it doesn't sound like she's drunk this time," Marigold offered with a shrug. Even so, her brain was reeling with how to get office-ready as quickly as possible. "But she has appeared at McClancy-Jansen and she's insisting on meeting with me."

"You took the day off of work." Elle frowned.

"Yeah. Well…" Marigold needed to at least throw a blazer over the shaker-stitch knit set she was wearing. And swap out some actual shoes for the fuzzy slippers on her feet. She didn't have time to explain her choices to Elle in the moment.

"You've gotta put that girl in her place. This is ridiculous." Elle shook her head. "You know Constance would never have stood for this crap. She taught you better."

Marigold's stomach twisted as she dropped her keys and wallet into her big purse. Between the debacles of falling for Kasima, the Ava situation, and her guilt over the time she'd lost with Constance, she had a lot of sour feelings swirling around inside her. Something was going to have to give.

"I know. And don't think it doesn't make me want to scream. But Allison has made her stance on this very clear. I'm not to do anything that would jeopardize the firm keeping Ava as a client."

"Then go," Elle conceded. "But this isn't how you handle your other clients, and McClancy-Jansen has never had a complaint about your methods before. You're damn good at your job, and that's why they put you on Ava's team in the first place. Stop doubting yourself. It's time to do that thing you do."

Tough love. It was the kind of thing that came with a friendship that had lasted decades, and Marigold was grateful for it. "Thanks for the pep talk." She gave Elle an impulsive hug before heading toward the door. "I've got to run. The entertainment world needs me. Lock up on your way out, okay?"

* * *

Georgette met Marigold at the elevators and got her up to speed as she ushered her into the office. "They're in the big conference room. Allison had me order in some food to distract them while we waited for you to arrive."

"Who's they? I thought it was Ava Ashford wanting to meet with me?"

"Yeah, well…" They had reached the end of the corridor and Georgette dramatically swept an open arm toward the floor-to-ceiling glass wall of the conference room. "She brought some friends."

Marigold rolled her lips to keep from grimacing. If she could see them, they could see her too. But, damn, order in some food was an understatement. The long, mahogany conference table was littered with discarded takeout containers, empty soda cans, and brown paper sacks that the food had apparently arrived in. Four young people besides Ava were in the room, all no doubt much too busy showing off for each other to worry about who might be observing them. Two were lounging across the less littered end of the table while making out, but the other two seemed to be vying for Ava's attention. One was dancing provocatively to the pop music blaring from a portable speaker, occasionally grinding up on Ava or grabbing her hand to spin her. The other had drawn a rather elaborate image of three demons on the whiteboard along with some sexually explicit phrases that were certainly not part of any image management campaign McClancy-Jansen was launching.

"Let me guess." She peered over at Georgette. "She keeps referring to this bunch as her entourage."

Georgette's lips curved upward like she was holding back a giggle. "How did you know?"

"This isn't my first time at the Ava Ashford entourage rodeo."

She had to stop that—making Wild West references when talking about her client. Just because Ava seemed to blur the lines between her on-screen persona and her actual identity didn't mean she should encourage it. Maybe that was part of the problem they had. Based on Ava's antics of late, she should actually focus a little more on widening that gap between fact and fiction.

"Thanks, Georgette. I'll take it from here."

She'd had the whole ride in from her house to the office to think it through, but it wasn't until that split second that she decided how she was going to play this. The tabletop love fest, the unnecessarily abundant amount of food, including the waste left behind for someone else to clean up, and that explicit sketch. The more she looked at the biggest demon in it, the harder it was to ignore the striking similarities to her own curly hair and curvy figure. Elle was right. Ava Ashford was a brat with a capital B, and she needed to be put in her place. Marigold was not doing her or her career any favors by listening to Allison and letting the poor behavior slide.

She slammed the conference room door shut behind her and cleared her throat loudly. As five pairs of eyes looked up at her, she strode across the room and disabled the speaker to stop the eardrum-shattering music. "My client has asked for a meeting with me, so I'm going to have to ask the rest of you to leave. You can wait quietly in the lobby if you'd like, but if you can't behave appropriately in our professional office, security will be called to remove you."

"It's okay. They're with me," Ava protested while the others chimed in with a whiny chorus made up of various iterations of "Don't be a drag, man."

"Leave," Marigold repeated louder in her best no-nonsense, Constance-inspired voice, and this time the four superfluous members of the group obeyed and scrambled out of the room.

"Why the hell did you do that?" Ava's face was a mask of disgust. Very unbecoming for a rising star.

"Why the hell did you have my boss call me into the office?" Marigold countered. If this kid thought throwing around a few swear words was going to make her back down, she had another think coming. "We did not have a meeting scheduled. This was supposed to be my day off and I had to come down here for what? To babysit while you and your make-believe entourage have an after-school pizza party?"

Ava's eyes went wide before hardening again. "I wanted to meet with you because I had a great idea for my next career step, although thanks to you it's probably all ruined."

"I ruined the next step in your career." Marigold resisted the urge to roll her eyes at the dramatics and stood firm with her hands on her hips. She wasn't about to fall victim to this pouty teenager crap. "How exactly did I do that?"

"My friends and I think it would be dope to pitch a reality TV show about us. You know, mostly about me, but they'd be a part of it too. A slice-of-life kind of thing or whatever." Ava's expression had softened as she began to talk about the plan, but then the sneer resurfaced. "Of course, now that you kicked them out and embarrassed me in front of them, they'll probably want nothing to do with me."

"Thank heaven for small miracles." Marigold was miles past hiding her true thoughts on the subject. "You didn't think that discussion could wait twenty-four hours until I was in the office again?"

"Well, I didn't think you'd be so uncool about it," Ava shot back.

"That's right. I'm so uncool. All I ever want to do are boring things that are in my client's best interest." Marigold remained impassive. "What are you suggesting the show would be about? The five of you sitting around eating takeout and being disrespectful to the people who purchased it for you?" She gestured from the mess on the table to the whiteboard. "Or mainly just you being rude and inconsiderate to the one person who is working to keep your career on track while still catering to your every whim, day off be damned."

"Hey, when McClancy-Jansen switched me to you as my manager, you said you'd be available for me twenty-four seven."

"I *am* available for you twenty-four seven—for *emergencies*," Marigold retorted. "And God knows, between the trashed hotel rooms and drunk and disorderly arrests, there have been enough of them."

"I wasn't arrested, just taken to the station. No harm, no foul." Ava's face was beet-red with anger now. Was she so accustomed to getting her way that she couldn't bear to take responsibility for her bad behavior?

What was with people lately? No one seemed to realize these days that their behavior impacted others. Didn't they know they couldn't just go through life jerking people around? Expecting others to rescue them from their bad choices, like Ava. Or dragging others into wacky schemes to lie to their family. Whatever. It was unacceptable, and Marigold wasn't having any more of it.

"We can schedule a time to meet next week to discuss the next steps for your career. I've already been working on some ideas I want to present to you." Marigold held up her hand to stop Ava from protesting the wait. "But no network is going to air the reality show you just pitched, so you're going to have to let it go."

"You're wrong."

"I'm not wrong." Marigold shook her head. "I've been in this business a long time and I know what I'm talking about."

"You're just jealous of me," Ava spat. "You're trying to force me to make the choices you would make. Like you're living through me or something. Last I heard, your acting career died decades ago, so what the hell do you know anyway?"

She may as well have slapped Marigold across the face. The sting didn't come from the sentiment behind the words—she'd dealt with angry clients before. Rather it was the familiarity of them. They were remarkably similar to what she'd said to Constance back when she fired her as her manager.

Of course, now with some time and distance, Marigold could see how it was less about Constance attempting to live through her or boss her around for fun and more about her merely trying to manage a young actor's career the best she could. Marigold could have handled her end of the deal with a little more grace, but the folly of youth had won out. That might be what would happen now with Ava, and there was a very real possibility that there was nothing she could do but watch it happen.

She took a deep breath before addressing Ava again. Calmness was key. She might lose Ava from her roster, but she needed to keep her from firing McClancy-Jansen all together.

"You have to know I'm only thinking of your career here and what's best for you as far as longevity in the business. But if you don't want my guidance, I'm sure someone else here at the firm can step in."

"That," Ava snapped. "That is what I want because this"—she gestured in Marigold's general direction—"is not working for me."

In her heart she'd hoped Ava would back down, but there it was—she was being dismissed by her client. Allison would not be pleased that she'd failed to handle the situation, but at least Ava wasn't walking away from the firm. Yet. She wouldn't leave Ava unattended and give her the chance to do so. She tapped out a quick IM to Allison. "Ms. Jansen will be in shortly to discuss what exactly you're looking for and offer some options for moving forward."

Fortunately, Allison was available and entered the conference room only moments later, saving them from the angry silence that had settled between them. Marigold excused herself and left her boss to salvage the situation. Between the disaster with Kasima the night before, the memory resurfacing of how she'd treated Constance in the past, and now losing a client, she was beat. It was all too much. She was halfway down the corridor before she realized she was blinking back tears.

CHAPTER TWENTY-SEVEN

Kasima sat in her office and skimmed the email from her brother with the facts and figures on Hooray For Howlywood sales. Marigold's live event plan had done the trick. After only two days of sales, they had already sold thirty-five percent of their stock. The news should have made her feel happy—and she was glad for SoCal Wildlife Rescue. But she didn't feel the joy and pride she usually did when one of her brews took off. She should be celebrating the victory with Marigold. It was her success as much as Kasima's. Enchanted Hops would have never been able to pull off this launch without her.

After Marigold had left the party Thursday night, Kasima had done her best to keep her game face on. The guilt that soured her stomach when she saw Marigold's stricken expression had quickly spiraled into hurt. Marigold hadn't even given her a chance to explain. She had never meant to do anything to make Marigold look bad. Or to hurt her. The entire basis for her keeping up the facade about their relationship long after she'd promised to come clean was to avoid disappointing her family. She was only trying to delay seeing that pitiful worried look return to her parents' faces again. That look that said, "Poor Kasima. Will she ever be okay again?"

Her parents had shown her a little grace and not questioned her while they were wrapping up the live launch Thursday night. Since she had had the day off from work on Friday, she'd managed to further avoid all family members, though she had to ignore several texts and phone calls. Her luck ran out Saturday morning when she'd decided to come into the office to try to catch up on work. She was way behind on planning the next brew series. But once in her office that morning, she'd gotten sidetracked checking her email, and the next thing she knew, her dad was peeking in through her office door.

"Hey, honey. How are you doing?" There it was in his eyes—all the pity and worry one person could carry.

"I'm fine, Dad," she lied. "Just trying to come up with a theme for the next series."

He shut the door behind him and sat tentatively in the chair opposite her desk. "It's Saturday and you're holed up in your office. Throwing yourself into your work just like you did after…" He sighed and rubbed his chin. "It's obvious you're upset about your breakup with Marigold. Want to talk about it?"

"Dad, Marigold and I didn't break up," she began.

"Kas, I was there. I saw it happen—Marigold even left the party early." His brow furrowed like he was trying to work something out. "Did the two of you make up? Is that why nobody heard from you yesterday?"

She didn't miss the dig about how she'd ignored everyone's messages, but the hopeful look in his eyes made Kasima's stomach twist. It was time to finally tell the truth. She looked down at her feet, shame burning her cheeks.

"No. We didn't break up because we were never together. Marigold wasn't really my girlfriend. We weren't even really dating." She breathed in and out, praying she could keep the tears at bay until she got through everything she needed to say. "I asked her to be my date for the SoCal Wildlife Rescue fundraiser because I couldn't stand to see all your worried faces when I was at another event alone. Then you referred to her as my girlfriend and I didn't correct you. Everything just snowballed from there."

"Kasima..." It was the softness in her dad's voice that gave the tears Kasima had been holding back permission to slide down her face.

When she met his gaze, she didn't see the anger she'd expected because she'd lied to him. Instead, sadness was written all over his face. Different, yet so much worse than the times she'd shown up to events dateless. Knowing her actions had caused it was like a punch to the gut.

"I was only trying to stop you and Mom from worrying about me, but misleading you wasn't the right way to do it. I get that now. I'm so sorry I lied to you."

"Oh, honey," he said as he pulled her into his arms, responding to her confession with grace and forgiveness. "You don't have to be anything other than yourself for us. You should know that. And I'm sorry that we gave you the impression we were expecting something else. Of course your mom and I worry about you. That's our job as parents. But we also know you're a strong, intelligent woman who is quite capable on your own."

It was the unconditional love her family had always provided, and she was grateful for that.

"Thanks, Dad." She sniffed and swiped away the tears on her face with her hand.

If only she could make things right with Marigold too, maybe she could put this whole debacle behind her. But Marigold seemed to have taken a page out of Kasima's own playbook and wasn't taking calls or returning any texts. Kasima wasn't able to apologize properly to her. She couldn't thank her for her help in the Hooray For Howlywood launch or celebrate that success with her. On top of that, over the past few months she'd become so comfortable with the back-and-forth communication between them during the day, she felt a real emptiness without it. She missed the little jokes they shared and the way she could bounce ideas off Marigold and get solid advice. She missed the cozy way they would curl up on the couch in front of the TV and Marigold would tell her about her day. She missed Marigold.

All of her efforts to guard her heart had failed. She'd lied to her family and to Marigold, and it turned out she'd been lying to herself too. She'd done her best to keep Marigold at arm's length and romance out of her life, but it didn't matter—her heart was broken anyway.

* * *

Kasima continued to hide out in her office that afternoon, but when her stomach started growling for substantial sustenance, she was reminded that she hadn't eaten anything since breakfast. She accepted the fact that inspiration was not going to strike. She needed something fresh and fun for the summer release to reflect that time of the year—summer fun, good times, and the perfect craft beer to go along with it all. But she was starting to worry she would never capture that vibe with the mood she was in. It was time to surrender for the day.

Normally, when she worked on a Saturday, she would just scoot over to the taproom and eat something there, but not feeling up to socializing, she left the brewery altogether. That was what led her to be wandering through the grocery store, humming along to the '80s-themed piped-in muzak. It had taken her the better part of the song for her to identify "Cum on Feel the Noize" absent the drums and vocals, but now that she had, the catchy tune would probably be stuck in her head the rest of the day. The music of the '80s was like that—it stuck with you.

While she perused the cheeses searching for the perfect selection to make a gloriously gooey, comforting sandwich, the song changed and a tinny version of the opening notes of Simple Minds's "Don't You (Forget About Me)" had her singing out loud, "Hey, hey, hey hey!"

Her mind was pulled back to the tequila-filled Sunday funday on her roof when Marigold suggested Don't Brew Forget About Me as a beer name. How long was that going to happen—Marigold randomly popping up in her subconscious? Despite the heavy feeling that had been accompanying her Marigold thoughts lately, she laughed under her breath. With all the margaritas they'd had that day, the discussion they'd had about naming beers had somehow been pushed to a far corner of her mind. She shook her head and reached for a wedge of Gruyere. That had been such a terrible beer name.

It suddenly hit her—the name was terrible, but the idea was a good one. Movies of the '80s were totally known for their fun vibe, and music from that era was still beloved by all generations. A nod to the music of those movies would be a great theme for the summer release.

She grabbed another hunk of cheese and a fresh loaf of Italian bread and headed toward the checkout. She went through the motion of purchasing her groceries and driving home, basically on autopilot, while her mind raced with a plan. She would use Marigold's *When Harry Met Sally* idea and brew an IPA with notes of green tea and vanilla—scents and flavors that she would always associate with Marigold. A tribute to the brain behind the beer name. It was the least she could do.

As she pulled her Jeep into the garage, she still felt that heady feeling of grabbing hold of inspiration and a problem solved, but she also had tears dampening her cheeks. Marigold wasn't returning her messages. It was clear she didn't want anything to do with her now, and Kasima couldn't deny that it hurt. She also couldn't deny that she only had herself to blame for their rift. She could have handled things better. She should have, at least. The heavy heart would be a reminder of the lesson learned. It sucked, but that was the way it was.

CHAPTER TWENTY-EIGHT

Marigold sat across the table from her while Constance worked a crossword puzzle in the rec room of Juniper Hills. The late-afternoon hours leading to dinner were quiet times at the living facility and one of her favorite times to visit. Many of the residents were gathered around the television, several appearing to doze off, while an entertainment news program hopped from one celebrity story to the next.

Suddenly Ava Ashford's smiling face filled the screen. Marigold wasn't surprised—the Internet was still abuzz about the *Homestead Hollow* finale and speculating about next season. It was no wonder the networks were trying to grab their share of the action.

Marigold was genuinely happy for Ava and the momentum her Dakota Oakley role was giving her career. Sometimes an agent-talent pairing just didn't click—it was part of the gig. Allison had reassigned Ava to Ethan, one of the up-and-comers at McClancy-Jansen, and he seemed to be doing fine by her. Getting this happy talk feature on the entertainment news program was certainly a step in the right direction. Ava should be pleased with the change in management.

Ethan was no doubt earning his commission trying to keep his new client happy, though. A smile tickled Marigold's lips as she recalled him looking slightly tortured earlier that afternoon as he followed Allison through the McClancy-Jansen office, apparently on the receiving end of the "kid-glove treatment" lecture.

It seemed like only days ago she and Kasima had been curled up together on the couch watching that last *Homestead Hollow* episode instead of nearly a whole month. Hell, two weeks had already gone by since the Hooray For Howlywood launch. Two weeks since the last time she had talked to Kasima. At first she'd been much too angry to respond to Kasima's calls and texts, but as the days went by that anger had faded. Her embarrassment about being a part of deceiving the Powells remained, however. Eventually the texts from Kasima had stopped, of course, and that was the end of it.

"Did you come here to visit with me or just to watch TV?"

"What?" Marigold swiveled in her chair to face Constance again. "Visit you. Of course. Sorry."

"Client of yours?" Constance nodded at the screen.

"Yes," she said out of habit before correcting herself. "I mean, no. Not anymore." She shook her head. She didn't want to spend their visit whining about her work. Not when Constance seemed to be having one of her good days.

It was exactly the kind of good day Marigold had been waiting for. She'd been thinking a lot about what Kasima had said the night they watched the *Homestead Hollow* finale—about how her feelings regarding the way she had treated Constance in the past were weighing her down. Without the constant emergency spin sessions needed to keep Ava's career on track and more free time on her hands since she wasn't hanging out with Kasima anymore, she'd had the chance to really turn that over in her mind. She needed to show herself some grace. Letting go of that burden, in her mind, required apologizing for her mistakes. Constance was the only family she had. She should do everything she could to heal their relationship and help them to make the most of the time they had together—good days and bad. She swallowed hard. This could go well or it could be a disaster, but she had to try.

"Constance, there's actually something I've been wanting to talk about with you."

"About the client that was a client, but isn't anymore?" Constance regarded her with eyes full of concern. "Is everything okay at work?"

"Oh, yes. Work's...great." Marigold instantly regretted the lie. Allison was still giving her the cold shoulder when they crossed paths in the office. It was like she was waiting to see that the Ethan-Ava pairing was going to work out before she rendered her verdict regarding Marigold's failing. "It's fine. Work's fine. Anyway, that's not what I wanted to talk about. I want to talk about what happened between us when I was a teenager. I want to apologize to you and—"

"No, no, no, Marigold. You don't have to do that." Constance shook her head and reached across the table to grasp her hand. "We both did things and said things we regret, I'm sure. But I was the adult—I'm your *mother*. I should've done better by you back then. Stood up for you better. Or maybe stood up *to* you better." She laughed and her eyes shone with tears—happy or sad, Marigold wasn't entirely certain.

"You were such a good manager." She felt the sting of tears in her own eyes. The feeling was catching apparently. "I want you to know that I think that all the time when I'm working. I...I model a lot of my managing style based on the way you handled my career."

This time Constance released a howl of laughter, causing one of the residents in front of the TV to mutter grumpily for them to hush.

"I hope you're not basing too much of your style on me. You're the only client I ever had, and I made plenty of mistakes."

"You did plenty right too," Marigold insisted. "You were a great example. As a manager and a mother. You were such a strong, independent woman. I looked up to you, even if I was too far into my stubborn teenage era to say so back then."

"Sometimes I worry that you picked up some of my not-so-great qualities. I'm afraid I didn't always set the best example for you. Especially when it came to keeping a healthy work-life balance."

"You were a single mom. You had a lot on your plate."

"After your dad left us, I threw myself into work. I made managing your career my entire life. I set those strict rules in place for you and for me. I thought they would keep everything neat and tidy. I allowed myself no personal life, and while I loved working with you, you were probably right—I was living vicariously through you in many ways. So much so, that I kind of lost myself. When I met Jeffery, it was like waking up from a long sleep. I realized how important those connections are. There's more to life than work—you need to cut loose every now and again. That's what makes the hard work worthwhile."

Marigold's chest tingled with a feeling she couldn't quite name. It wasn't just the revelation that Constance had just shared with her, but also the entire conversation that they were having. They had filled most of their visits with chit-chat about the minutia of their days, never really connecting like this. And it was all happening because Kasima had encouraged her to talk to Constance about how she was feeling.

"You have no idea how badly I needed to hear that."

"I have some idea. I noticed how your face lit up when you talked about your new friend." Constance gave her a knowing look. "And how you've stopped mentioning her altogether the past couple of weeks. And I also understand that you have a job that you're very good at and that you probably need to take that call."

Marigold glanced down at her buzzing phone, hopeful that it would be Kasima's name that showed on the screen, but of course it wasn't. The name that flashed was surprising nonetheless: Ava Ashford.

"It's okay," Constance said. "Take the call. I have places to be too, you know." She gestured at the other residents, who were leaving their seats in front of the TV to shuffle off in the direction of the dining room. "It's dinner time and word on the street is they're serving Italian wedding soup instead of split pea tonight. Life is good. See you in a few days." She kissed Marigold on the top of the head before following the others out of the room.

Left alone in the Juniper Hills rec room, the talking heads on the TV the only noise in the place, her mind was still spinning. Did she really just have that conversation with Constance? Advice on both her career and her personal life was the last thing she'd expected from the visit and yet…that was exactly what she'd received. Better than any of that, for the first time in decades she felt hopeful about her relationship with her mother.

A swipe of her phone screen revealed she'd actually missed two phone calls from Ava. She clicked on the voice mail left after the second attempt to reach her.

"Marigold, I need your help…*please*." Ava's voice sounded little—like a much younger girl rather than too-big-for-her-britches Dakota Oakley—and as frustrated as Marigold still felt with her ex-client, the plea melted her heart enough to warrant a call back.

* * *

Marigold swallowed down the "I told you so" on her lips as she pulled up to Ava's grandmother's house. Ava had explained the situation when Marigold returned her call, but even as she approached the front door, she could tell things were much worse than she'd been led to believe.

Ava met her on the front porch with red-rimmed eyes that indicated a good cry, a bad hangover, or a desperate lack of sleep. Quite possibly all three. "Thank you for coming. I didn't know who else to call."

"Tell me again why you didn't call Ethan?" Marigold frowned, worried that her coworker would accuse her of stepping on his toes. "He's your manager now, you know."

"He said this was more of a personal problem and less of a talent management problem."

"It's definitely some kind of problem," Marigold muttered as she stepped into the Craftsman-style home's living room.

Just as Ava had told her earlier, her misguided decision to invite the ragtag bunch she called her entourage to live in the house with her to prove the living arrangement would make good

TV had gone seriously sideways. The scene was reminiscent of the hotel room she'd extracted Ava from a few months earlier—basically trashed, with an armchair upended, a coffee table littered with discarded takeout food containers, and empty beer bottles everywhere. The room had the distinct rank odor of stale liquor and humans who hadn't showered recently. Sprawled across the couch was one of the young people from the group—whether in a deep sleep or simply passed out for the moment, Marigold couldn't be certain.

"I can't believe your grandmother allowed you to do this."

"Well..." Ava bit her lip and looked everywhere but directly at Marigold. "She's not *exactly* here right now."

That was obviously not the whole story, but the loud crash that came from the kitchen urged Marigold to take action now, ask questions later. "We're going to talk about where *exactly* she is, so don't think that answer passed as even remotely satisfactory, but for now we need to take care of this situation. Dare I ask who—or what—is banging around in the kitchen?"

Marigold marched down the hall to answer the question but immediately regretted her choice of words. "Oh, my God!"

There on the kitchen table in a state of half-dress was the couple she'd previously seen making out in the McClancy-Jansen conference room going at it yet again, apparently completely oblivious—or more likely, uncaring—that they were not alone in the space.

"Stop it! Stop it, you two," she admonished the pair as she lunged for the spray nozzle of the kitchen sink faucet and blasted them with a stream of cold water. "Put your clothes back on. This is not your kitchen to fuck around in."

"What the hell," one of the two groused, holding up a hand to try to shield themselves from the water.

"Listen up, people who do not actually live in this house." Marigold's voice was loud enough to carry as she strode back down the hall to the living room. "You are being evicted. Get your stuff and get the hell out!"

Her booming alto had been enough to rouse the sleepyhead on the couch. He rubbed his forehead and glared at her. "You can't kick us out. Dakota Oakley invited us to stay."

Marigold shot Ava a withering look. Did these people even know her real name?"

"I've changed my mind," Ava mumbled.

"She's changed her mind," Marigold repeated in her most serious tone. "You're lucky I'm allowing you to get your stuff. Get moving before I call the cops."

"You don't scare me, lady." He sat up but seemed to regret the movement. He held his head in his hands as he continued, "You're her agent. You're not going to call the cops. She's underage and will be in as much trouble as any of us." He pointed accusingly at Ava.

"I've got news for you, my dude." Marigold shrugged. "I'm not her agent. She fired me weeks ago, so I've got nothing to lose here. And you have no idea what I'm willing to risk to get what I want." She yanked the front door open and gave an exaggerated wave. In a few short beats, two uniforms appeared on the stoop.

"Oh, crap." The kid scrambled off the couch and out of the room, presumably to gather his belongings.

"What's going on down here? Dakota, can you order us burgers? I have a hell of a—" The fourth member of the entourage appeared at the bottom of the staircase but stopped short at the scene in the living room.

"What's going on is *Ava* will no longer be buying you burgers, or beer, or anything else. She also will no longer be hosting this extended sleepover," Marigold said before raising her voice to be heard in the kitchen as well. "That goes for you two as well, lovebirds. You can leave on your own, or I can have these officers escort you out. That's up to you. But either way, you've got to go. Now."

To her relief, all four of the interlopers had pushed past the uniforms in the doorway and left the house before a full five minutes had passed.

The moment they were gone, one of the officers slapped Marigold on the back. "You were right, it worked."

"I owe you one." Marigold grinned back at her before turning to Ava. "This is my friend Elle Bissett and her neighbor Matthew."

"You're not actually police officers?" Ava gaped and relief crept into her expression. "So, I'm not in trouble?"

"I wouldn't say you're completely off the hook, but you're not going to get any grief from these two." Marigold nodded in her friends' direction.

After she sent the fake officers on their way, she surveyed the mess around them. Ethan was smart to set some boundaries and take a pass on answering Ava's call. But Marigold was hopeful that there was still a lesson to be learned in all of this. "Let's get this mess cleaned up, then you and I are going to have a little heart-to-heart."

To her surprise, Ava didn't protest. She just got to work.

* * *

It was two stuffed trash bags later when the two of them finally sat down in the kitchen. Marigold pushed a tall glass of water across the table to Ava. "You look like you could use this. Just because the show's on hiatus doesn't mean you should stop taking care of yourself, you know."

"I know," Ava said between gulps of water. "Things just got a little out of hand."

"A little out of hand," Marigold repeated slowly, looking from the sink full of dirty dishes to the weird, sticky puddle on the floor next to the garbage can. There was no way any of this would fly with Anita Ashford. "That may be putting it a little mildly. When is your grandmother coming back?"

Ava chewed her bottom lip and her eyes filled with tears.

What was going on with this kid? "Hey." Marigold put a comforting hand on Ava's forearm. "Is everything okay? Is your.... grandmother okay?"

Mopping her face with her sleeve, Ava managed a nod. "She's fine, but she's not coming back. At least not any time soon."

"What are you talking about? Where did she go?" Marigold's confusion grew as Ava pulled away and crossed her arms. At least she was starting to look more like her headstrong self—the defiant client who broke off their working relationship just a couple of weeks ago. She didn't have to be there—she didn't have to help Ava at all. But still, when she remembered that small voice on the phone message, her heart tugged again. "You asked me to help you, and I showed up. I got those freeloaders out of your house, and I can help you get this place cleaned up, but you've got to tell me the truth about what's going on."

"Grandma had a stroke."

Marigold caught her gasp before it escaped her. Obviously the situation was stressful enough for Ava without an overly dramatic reaction to the news. "I'm so sorry to hear that. When did this happen?"

There was more lip chewing before Ava responded, "About five months ago."

"Five months ago," Marigold echoed as the pieces fell into place for her. That would have been right around when Ava's behavior shifted from congenial and compliant to more reckless and defiant. "I'm guessing her recovery has been slow going."

Ava nodded. "She needs a lot of care still. More than I would be able to handle. Eventually she may be able to come home and we can get her in-home care, but for now she's staying in a care facility called Juniper Hills. So, I've been on my own. And I guess I suck at adulting."

Of course. Anita was living in the same facility as Constance. It *was* Ava whom Marigold had seen out front of the residence that day after all. Only she hadn't been following Marigold or had any other nefarious reason for being there—she was just visiting her grandmother.

"I'm familiar with the facility." Why wasn't she being honest with Ava after she'd asked her for the truth? Marigold recalled Constance's advice from earlier about connecting with people. Why was she still holding back? Ava technically wasn't her client anymore, but she did still feel compelled to help her. Maybe sharing her experience would help ease some of Ava's anxiety about the situation. "I'm actually very familiar with Juniper Hills—my mother lives there. She suffered a brain injury a few years back. The residence is clean, well-managed, and the staff is top-notch. Your grandmother is in good hands."

"I know," Ava sniffed. "But I feel like I should be doing more for her. Taking care of her or something."

"If she needs medical care on the daily, then she's where she needs to be for now. What you can do is take care of yourself and take better care of the house and keep your career on track. That's what your grandmother would want you to do. And as far as the adulting part? I can get you set up with a good cleaning service and maybe offer a little advice on how to keep things running smoothly around here. But you have to promise me you're done with the entourage for real this time. Stop picking up random sycophants in bars. Make some real connections." The echo of Constance's words was not lost on her, but they rang true in this instance as well.

"I promise." Ava smiled for the first time since Marigold walked through the door. "You were right about them. I should've listened to you in the first place. And I never should've fired you. I'm really sorry about that. I like Ethan enough, but I want to come back to you. Will you be my manager again?"

"I...don't think that's a good idea." Marigold shook her head.

"Why not?"

"I don't want to step on Ethan's toes for one, but more than that, it's not good for your career to keep jumping managers. I've talked to Ethan, and he has some good ideas for you. I think you should give him a chance to put them in motion."

"Okay." Ava gave her a shaky smile. "If you think that's best."

"I do," Marigold confirmed. Ethan would do right by Ava as long as she listened to him, and Marigold had a good feeling about that now. She believed Ava had finally turned a corner. The kid was going to be all right.

Marigold's chest filled with pride knowing that it was due, at least in part, to the connection she'd forged between them. Maybe it was time to strengthen some other connections in her life as well—see what other good things were out there for her.

"Of course, that doesn't mean we can't be friends."

CHAPTER TWENTY-NINE

"The party can start, the grape soda has arrived," Kasima announced as she entered her brother's house, where her family had gathered to celebrate Matty's inline hockey victory. She found the group in the kitchen along with enough pizza and wings to feed an entire team despite the fact that it was only the six of them dining. "Along with your favorite aunt."

Matty abandoned his plate and bounded across the room to hug her. "Did you see my goal, Aunt Kas?"

"I sure did. You were on fire out there. And don't think I missed the way you checked that forward at the end of the first period. You're getting to be a real bruiser." She gave him a teasing elbow to the ribs, and he beamed back at her with pride.

"Where's Marigold?" He took one of the bottles of grape soda from the carrier in her hand. "I thought maybe she'd come with you."

"Oh, no. She, uh…" She cast a pleading glance in Spencer's direction, hoping he would rescue her. She'd come clean to the rest of her family about not actually being Marigold's girlfriend, but having to tell her eight-year-old nephew that she'd been lying to everyone felt especially shameful. Maybe Marigold had been on to something with her insistence about not lying to her family.

"Hey, kiddo. Pizza's getting cold." Spencer took the hint and directed his son back to the table, but he followed Kasima to the fridge where she found a spot for the soda. "You're not the only one who's missing her."

"What?" She helped herself to an IPA.

"You're obviously missing Marigold. It's okay to admit it. We all liked her."

"No, I'm fine. Really." She moved to step around him, but he blocked her escape. "I'm just trying to join in the victory dinner."

He wasn't swayed. "I've known you your entire life." He lowered his voice to keep the conversation just between them. "I can tell you've been sad since the two of you stopped hanging out. You miss her. And I saw how you were together. You had real feelings for her whether you want to admit it or not. It was obvious she liked you too. So what the hell are you doing?"

Why was he pushing her on this?

"I tried to both call her and text her to apologize, but she didn't respond." She shook her head. He didn't get it. She'd tried to fix things between them, but Marigold wasn't interested. "I guess it just wasn't meant to be. It's fine."

He pulled a doubtful face. "You keep saying it's fine and you're fine, but I can't help but notice you crafted a beer inspired by her." When she rolled her eyes at him, he held up a hand to stop her. "Just because I'm a dude doesn't mean I don't recognize the scent of green tea. Marigold always smells like it. And you named the beer It Had To Be Brew, for God's sake."

"It's just a pun," she protested. "It was a joke we shared about a song from *When Harry Met Sally*, that's all."

"Okay. Listen, if you want to keep telling yourself this stuff because it's easier than taking a chance or whatever, that's fine." He put his hands up in surrender. "But if I were you, I wouldn't let her get away that easily. If you can't reach her by phone, maybe you should get your face in front of her *in person*. Who could resist this face?"

He reached to pinch her cheek, but this time she dodged him. She stuck her tongue out as she scooted away toward the rest of the family, but his point had been made. She might not want to admit to her big brother that he was right, but she did miss Marigold and she wanted another chance with her. But was it worth risking her heart again, or was it better to just play it safe and hope her feelings would pass?

CHAPTER THIRTY

Saturday morning Marigold propped herself up on a stool at her breakfast bar waiting for her coffee to brew. She'd been bone tired from their efforts to get Anita's house back in order, yet sleep had escaped her when she finally fell into her bed. Ava's predicament had distracted her from further contemplating her earlier conversation with Constance, but once home again, she was no longer able to avoid thinking about it. She'd tossed and turned all night, considering what Constance said to her about missing connections. The advice had served her well when dealing with Ava, but that was work-related. Or at least work-adjacent. Doing right by her clients had always come naturally to her. Personal connections—real relationships—not so much.

With Kasima, though, it had been easy. Being with her felt natural and comfortable. Not so comfortable that there wasn't an electricity between them. Kasima definitely made her lady parts buzz. Hell, Kasima made all her parts buzz. Then Marigold had to go and overreact about the little white lie they'd told and mess everything up. She'd been able to forgive Constance for insisting on subterfuge and deceit when she was managing Marigold's career, and that was thanks to encouragement from Kasima. Marigold knew in her heart that Kasima hadn't started the lie about them being in a relationship with any nefarious intent. She had simply been trying to spare her parents from worrying about her. Yeah. She had overreacted.

She added a heaping spoonful of sugar and a splash of cream to her coffee, wishing it was a blonde vanilla latte instead of something brewed from a pod, but caffeine was caffeine. She needed to clear her head and figure out what to do—how to apologize for everything. Would Kasima even want to hear it at this point? Her texts and calls had stopped weeks ago. Maybe Kasima wouldn't even want to talk to her again. That thought made her chest fill with a heaviness she could hardly bear, because if she was so concerned about the truth, she was going to have to come to grips with this one: she really cared about Kasima and she wasn't prepared to let her go.

She wasn't prepared to let Kasima go. And that was the truth.

Marigold swallowed a gulp of scalding-hot pod coffee and made up her mind. She would go to Kasima's and say it to her in person. Say that she was sorry about the way she'd acted and that they deserved a real chance to make this thing between them work. And she wouldn't wait any longer to do it.

Thirty minutes later, she was showered, dressed, fully caffeinated, and ready to go. That was when her doorbell rang.

She briefly considered ignoring the individual pressing the bell—until she caught a glimpse of a Jeep parked at the curb in front of her house.

Kasima's Jeep.

Her heart pounded as she hurried to the front door, and without even thinking about what she would say or why Kasima would be standing on her front stoop unannounced and with a six-pack of beer in her hands, she yanked the door open.

* * *

Kasima was not expecting Marigold to appear in the doorway so quickly, but there they were—suddenly face-to-face after not having talked in nearly a month. Marigold looked good in her flared jeans and mustard-yellow sleeveless chiffon top. *Were her shoulders always that sexy?* Every well-practiced word Kasima had intended to say vacated her brain, leaving her swallowing hard and blinking rapidly, desperate for a coherent string of syllables to come out of her mouth. "I have something I want to say to you." *Whelp, it was coherent.*

"Okay," Marigold said tentatively. "I have something to say to you too."

"Please let me go first." She couldn't lose her momentum. She had to say the thing she came here to say before she lost her nerve. "I'm sorry about the lying, I know it was the wrong thing to do. And I hate that my lies hurt you and ruined the good thing we had going. I…miss you."

"Well, I—"

"That's not all." Kasima had to keep pushing on. "I wasn't just lying to my family and you, I was lying to myself too. Because no matter how many times I said we could only be friends, or friends with benefits, the truth is I felt something deeper for you. I thought if I didn't admit it out loud it wouldn't be true, but my heart knew better. All in that time we spent getting to know each other, working together, sharing hopes and joys, and even some tough stuff about our fears, I was starting to fall in love with you. And I'm sorry I wasn't honest with you or with myself. I guess you can't protect a heart from something it wants so badly."

"Your heart wants to be with me?" Marigold stepped backward further into the house, and Kasima took that as a sign to follow her in.

She set the beer down and took Marigold's hands in hers. "Yes. I mean, *I* want to be with you. If you'll have me."

"Oh, my God." Marigold laughed and pulled her into her arms. A positive reaction, if not exactly the one Kasima had expected. "I was on my way to say the same thing to you. I want to be with you. I was coming to insist you give us a real chance to be together."

"Insist? So, that's a yes?" Kasima needed the reassurance. She wouldn't be totally relieved until she knew for certain that they were finally on the same page. Wanting the same thing—each other.

Marigold pulled back and their gazes locked. "That is one hundred percent, without a doubt, a yes."

Kasima's held breath barely had time to release before their mouths crashed together in a kiss that left no question about how Marigold felt. "Yes, right back at ya," she murmured against Marigold's lips.

When they finally broke apart again, Marigold glanced over at the six-pack Kasima had carried in. "Was your original plan to get me drunk to get me to say yes to you?"

"Wait, would that have worked?"

"I am partial to Enchanted Hops Brewing Company beer, so…"

"But wait," Kasima said as she reached for one of the cans. "This isn't just any beer. This is a beer inspired by the woman who has turned my world completely upside down. And it's called…" She thrust the can out dramatically. "It Had To Be Brew. It's basically an IPA, just with a little something extra."

"It Had To Be Brew?" Marigold took the can and squinted at the label. "Like, 'It Had to Be You'? You used my idea—modern movie songs?"

"I did. It's a series of four beers, including Haze-y Shade of Summer, which is a play on—" Kasima closed her eyes and took a breath. The beer names weren't the important thing here, and despite the twinkle in Marigold's eye that always appeared when she talked excitedly about her product, she needed to keep things on track. "You know what? You can read the names on the other cans later. But this one had to be brewed because, for me, it had to be you."

Marigold appeared to bite back an amused grin and studied the can more closely before reading the description aloud, "A bold IPA with notes of green tea and vanilla. That sounds yummy."

"And irresistible. Just like you," Kasima said before taking Marigold in her arms and kissing her again, sealing the promise that going forward everything between them was very, very real.

ONE YEAR LATER

Marigold fussed with the floral centerpiece on the rustic wooden table in the backyard before stepping back to take in the tablescape as a whole. Kasima had strung fairy lights everywhere, making the space seem romantic and absolutely magical. Their backyard looked perfect and perfect was exactly what she wanted for this dinner party. It was the first time they were hosting the Powells and Constance in their home.

Their home. Because three months earlier, Kasima had moved in with her. Now the vibrant artwork created by Libby hung on the bungalow walls, and though Kasima had given up her rooftop oasis in Echo Park, she had moved her teak table and U-shaped sofa to the low deck behind the house accessible through the French doors leading from their bedroom. Their own private haven. They were officially in a very real, very romantic relationship. That wasn't the only thing that had changed in the past year.

Constance was still residing at Juniper Hills as she was still in need of the care, but since their mother-daughter breakthrough a year earlier, she and Marigold were making the most of her good days. Marigold had even been bringing Constance to their house once a month instead of hanging out with her in the Juniper Hills rec room. Kasima would let the two visit while she prepared a meal for them all to share—and it was never, ever split pea soup.

Ava Ashford had made some changes in the past year as well. She'd kept her promise and dropped the entourage of randoms, an act that may or may not have been strongly influenced by her grandmother returning home after her recovery was complete. Shortly before Christmas, her agent, Ethan, had left McClancy-Jansen to hang out a shingle of his own, but Ava had stayed with the agency. After months of building a connection as a mentor/mentee and as friends, Ava was back on Marigold's good side as well as on her client roster. That past spring she had won a People's Choice Award for her role as Dakota Oakley and was currently filming the third season of *Homestead Hollow*. Once the show went on hiatus, she was scheduled to shoot her first feature film, in which she had a leading role. At last, she truly was the big freaking deal she was always telling people she was.

"Hey, babe." Kasima's voice from the deck brought Marigold's focus back to the present. "Everything ready out here? My family will be here any minute now, and you know they'll come hungry."

"Constance okay in there?"

"She's watching a *Murder She Wrote* rerun. She's fine." Kasima looked radiant standing in the sunshine, skin glowing, hair back in braids, wearing khaki cargo shorts and a simple pale-pink T-shirt. She really was Marigold's dream girl.

Marigold had never been happier than she'd been in the past year, and she had a giddy, floaty feeling that things were only going to get better. Maybe today was the day to pull out the diamond ring she'd carefully selected and finally pop the question. She would wait until their guests had left for the evening and it was just the two of them again.

"All set out here then. Let me just fix this…" She leaned over the center piece and fussed with the arrangement of the flowers one last time, but when she turned back around to go inside and greet their guests, Kasima was down on one knee holding out a wooden ring box engraved with a M and a K. "Oh, my God. Are you…?"

"Yes, I am." Kasima nodded and opened the box to reveal a large diamond flanked by two smaller sapphires. "Marigold Luxe, will you marry me?"

Marigold felt the sting of happy tears at the back of her eyes. "Kasima, I love you so very much. Yes. Yes, I will marry you." She pulled her into her arms and kissed her hard and firm to seal the promise.

When they finally broke apart again, Kasima slid the ring onto Marigold's finger. "I love you too."

Marigold took both of her hands. "You should know I have a ring in my nightstand that I picked out for you, because I was going to ask *you* to marry *me*."

"Well," Kasima said, with watery eyes. "I say 'yes' to you too." She called over her shoulder, "We said 'yes!'"

"Who are you talking to?"

Kasima just grinned at her as the whole Powell family, along with Constance, Elle, and Ashley, came out onto the deck cheering and applauding.

"Ah, okay." Marigold smiled and waved to everyone feeling very blessed. "Is that a boombox Spence is carrying?"

"It's my dad's."

"But why?"

Kasima didn't need to speak for Marigold to have her answer. Spencer set the boombox on the table and the opening strains of "We Are Family" played from the speakers.

"Family dance?" Marigold asked.

"Family dance," Kasima confirmed.

"Let's celebrate!" Brian's voice boomed as everyone moved to the lawn and eased into the choreography.

"Come on, family." Kasima linked arms with Marigold and dragged her right into the center of the group.

They all twirled and shimmied along to the song, and this time Marigold was able to keep up with every step. She'd had ample opportunities to learn the routine over the past year. Constance, Elle, and Ashley were doing their best to match the dance moves of the others. But one thing was clear, everyone was smiling and laughing, having a great time together.

Marigold looked at the faces around her with a full heart. She was surrounded by all the people she loved. Family. When the song ended and the group erupted into cheers again, she wrapped her arms around Kasima and kissed her on the lips.

"It's just like you always say." Marigold beamed at her. "It had to be brew."

Bella Books
Happy Endings Live Here
P.O. Box 10543
Tallahassee, FL 32302
Phone: (800) 729-4992
www.BellaBooks.com

More Titles from Bella Books

Jones – Gerri Hill
978-1-64247-598-2 | 260 pages | Mystery
One weekend getaway, six friends, and a deadly secret that will wash away everything they thought they knew.

Merry Weihnachten – E. J. Noyes
978-1-64247-610-1 | 292 pages | Romance
Christmas traditions aren't the only things getting mixed up when these two hearts collide beneath the mistletoe.

Sweet Home Alabarden Park – TJ O'Shea
978-1-64247-570-8 | 362 pages | Romance
She came to restore a royal estate—she never expected to rebuild her heart.

Dr. Margaret Morgan – Christy Hadfield
978-1-64247-628-6 | 286 pages | Romance
Facing the professor on campus everyone hates is terrifying—but falling for her might be even worse.

Overtime – Tracey Richardson
978-1-64247-630-9 | 278 pages | Romance
A charming romance about second chances, found family, and scoring the goal that matters most.

The Big Guilt – Renée J. Lukas
978-1-64247-657-6 | 206 pages | Romance
What if the one who got away became the one you can't have?

www.ingramcontent.com/pod-product-compliance
Lightning Source LLC
Jackson TN
JSHW022338110725
87454JS00001B/4
* 9 7 8 1 6 4 2 4 7 6 7 2 9 *